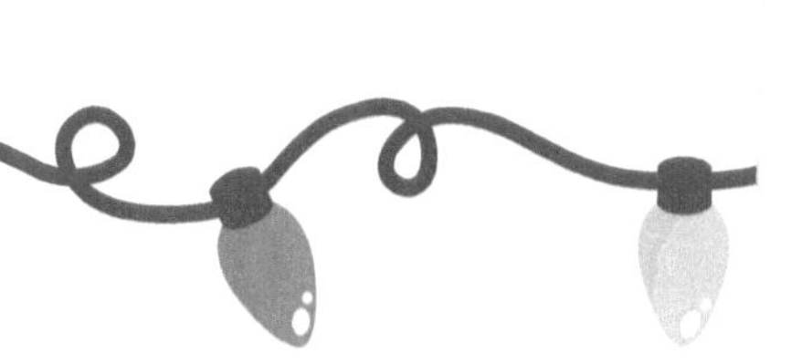

SNOWED

VI KEELAND
PENELOPE WARD

SNOWED
Cover designer: Sommer Stein, Perfect Pear Creative
Editing: Jessica Royer Ocken
Formatting and proofreading:
Elaine York, Allusion Publishing
Proofreading: Julia Griffis

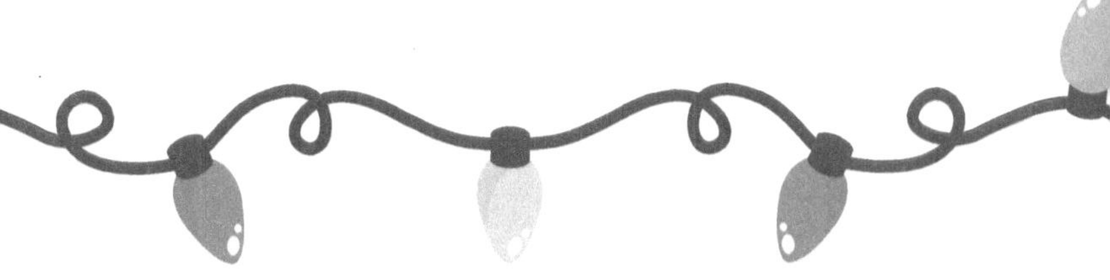

SNOWED

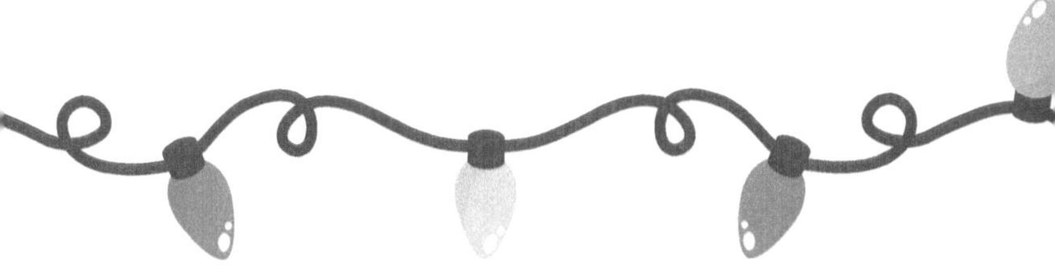

MERRY
INKMAS

CHAPTER 1

Daria

"You two need to cut the shit!" Billie pulled the door closed behind her and stepped into the reception area where Cade and I were arguing—yet again.

I wasn't about to say it, but this time it was sort of the boss's fault, since Billie had put us both on decorating duty after we finished our last appointments of the day. It was taking forever because we couldn't even agree on how to hang garland or decorate a tree.

"We can all hear you bickering. The clients included," she said. "Even over the sound of the tattoo machines."

My shoulders slumped. "Sorry, Billie."

"Don't be sorry. Just figure out how to be friends already. Okay?"

She waited until we both nodded to go back into the studio. As soon as the door shut again, I looked over at Cade and whispered, "It's still crooked, you idiot."

"It's not freaking crooked." He climbed down from the ladder, slapping dirt from his hands. "And who cares if it is? It's good enough."

"I do. *Billie* does. It's only a little more than a week until Christmas. Maybe dig deep for some holiday cheer." I brushed past him. "Just get out of the way. I'll fix it myself."

Cade McMahon and I had both started as tattoo artists at Billie's Ink two months ago, one week apart. We hadn't gotten along since my second day, when I'd unknowingly tatted one of his long-time clients. Things had gotten worse the last few weeks. If whoever makes those Grinch movies ever needed a new actor, Cade would be a shoo-in. No acting required. The man was grumpier by the day as we slid toward the twenty-fifth. I could tell Billie was at her wit's end. She probably wouldn't admit it, but I was certain the team-building retreat we were all required to attend this week up in Vermont was mainly because of me and Cade.

I climbed the ladder, removed the star from the artificial Christmas tree, and bent the top branch a little to the right before replacing it and leaning back for a look. "There," I said. "That wasn't so hard."

Cade frowned but said nothing for a change. I picked up the paper with the funky snow scene Billie had sketched. She wanted us to paint something similar on the shop's front window.

"I'll do the snowman and the snow," I said. "You paint the scenery in the background and then tat up Frosty."

He shrugged. "Whatever."

It took us another hour, but at least we didn't bicker—though that was probably only because neither of us ever said two words while we worked on art. I finished my part a few minutes before Cade, which gave me a chance to watch him in action. He held two thin paintbrushes between his teeth, and his head bopped along to whatever he had playing in his earbuds. It was really a shame the guy was a giant asshole, because he was also phenomenally good-looking. At least when he wasn't talking. Chiseled jawline, a perfect, straight nose, and plump lips that women paid big money for. *What a waste.*

Deek, another tattoo artist at Billie's, walked his last client of the day out from the back. The two shook hands.

"Merry Christmas, man."

Deek waved. "You too. I'll see you next month for the color fill-in."

The extra bells I'd hung at the top of the front door jingled as it opened and closed. Deek looked around the now-decorated reception area. "Nice job. And no blood shed, from what I can see. Maybe there's such a thing as a Christmas miracle after all."

He walked toward the door that separated the lobby from the studio. "Oh, I almost forgot. Change of plans for the trip up to Vermont tomorrow morning."

"Are we leaving later, I hope?" Cade asked.

"Nah. Bosslady still wants to get on the road by five. There's a big storm heading to Vermont. She wants to get to the cabin by the time the heavy stuff comes down. But there's a change in the carpools. I'm not riding with you anymore, Cade. Justine and I are going with Billie in her car. We decided to make a pit stop in Connecticut to visit Big Ed, a friend of ours who used to work here. He moved to L.A. a few years back, but he's in town visiting his parents. Their place is right on the way, off I-95."

"Can I still go with you guys?" I asked, feeling panicked.

Deek shook his head. "Billie wants you two to ride together. She doesn't want anyone riding alone."

"But..."

The boss suddenly walked out from the back with her client. I waited until he left to continue the conversation. "Deek was just telling us about the change in carpools tomorrow. I really don't think it's a good idea for Cade and me to spend seven hours in the car."

Billie put her hands on my shoulders. "I think it's *exactly* what you two need."

Deek looked at me and chuckled. "You look like I just told you you're being sent to the electric chair."

"I might prefer that," I mumbled.

"Oh, come on now," Billie said. "Think of all the fun we're going to have this weekend. We're going to go tubing, ice skating, make a big fire... I promise, Colby's parents' cabin is amazing."

I sulked. "I'd rather ride there with you guys."

Billie ignored me and spoke to Cade. "Can you fit two boxes in your trunk? Mine is small and will barely fit all of our bags."

Cade shrugged. He didn't look too happy about the new arrangements either. "Sure."

"Great. One is a box of board games. I read they're good for team building. I had Colby order them. I also let him pick them out, so I'm actually a little scared. My husband is a geek at heart. We may wind up playing something *Star Wars*-themed or Dungeons & Dragons. The Amazon box just came today. I haven't even opened it. The other box is liquor and mixers." She thumbed toward the back. "Let me grab them."

While Billie and Cade took stuff to his car, Deek and I sterilized all the equipment and loaded the autoclave chamber. As they came back in, Deek lifted his chin to me. "Hey. Give the guy a chance this weekend. There's a lot more to him than meets the eye."

I sighed. "Great. Just what I want. *More* Cade."

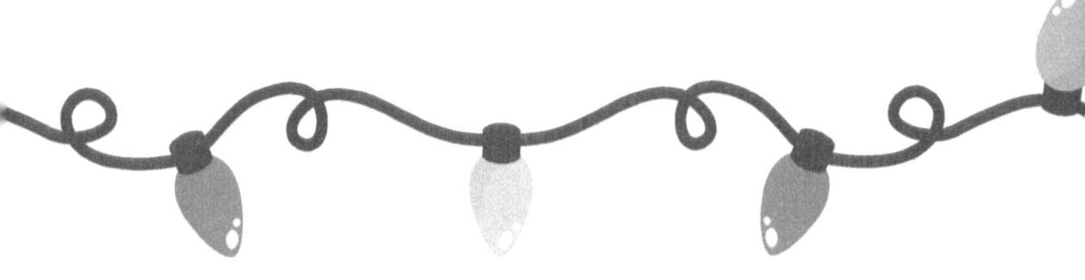

CHAPTER 1

Cade

Team building was off to a great start, if you counted Daria ignoring me the entire ride to Vermont while she listened to an audiobook. She had the thing playing so freaking loud that I could hear it through her headphones and over my music.

Snowflakes started to fly as we were about halfway to our destination. I hoped we didn't encounter much traffic, otherwise we stood a good chance of running into trouble on the icy roads.

At one point, I turned to her. "You want to stop for coffee? I could use the energy boost."

No response. She couldn't hear me because she had her volume up so loud.

A couple of minutes later, I raised my voice. "Do you want to stop for coffee?"

She jumped. "Damn! No need to yell."

"Well, you couldn't hear me before."

"I had the volume turned up higher for one scene. I didn't want to miss any of it. But I turned it back down."

"What was so important about it?"

She shook her head. "You wouldn't get it."

"Why?"

"It's a romance."

I arched a brow. "Oh, you're embarrassed because it's corny?"

"No, actually, I'm not ashamed of what I read at all. I just don't think you'll get it."

"Try me." I turned the windshield wipers on. "What was happening in that scene?"

"The hero just killed a guy for staring too long at the woman he cares about."

What the hell kind of shit is that? "That's a little fucked up." I chuckled.

"Well, he'd been stalking her for some time and invested a lot in their relationship. It pissed him off, so..."

"And that turns you on?"

"It's a dark romance—just fantasy. He offs people for other reasons, too. Not just when he's jealous."

"You fantasize about murderers..."

"Only imaginary ones."

"Here I was thinking you were listening to some soft romance like my grandmother used to read. Figures you have a dark and twisted side."

"You say that like it's a bad thing." She flashed a mischievous grin.

"I didn't say it was—it might even suit you."

"I'll take that as a compliment." She looked out her window. "And yes, I would like to stop for coffee."

I pointed to a sign we were about to pass. "There's an exit coming up. Dunkin' or Starbucks?"

"McDonald's."

I grimaced. "McDonald's?"

"Yeah."

"Not the first place I think of for coffee."

"Their coffee is just as good, and it's cheaper. Plus, I like their fries."

Five minutes later, we'd ordered coffee and fries from the McDonald's drive-thru—breakfast of champions—but it was slow as molasses getting to the pay window.

"Great." I sighed. "Now we're stuck in this long-ass drive-thru."

Daria turned to me. "Do you have somewhere else to be, Grumpypants? It's not like you've been looking forward to this weekend. Why the big rush?"

"I don't want to get stuck on the road in the freaking snowstorm that's coming."

"We won't get stuck," she insisted as we finally pulled up to the pay window.

I handed the attendant my card and told Daria, "If we do get stuck, I'm blaming you and your damn McDonald's."

"Don't get McMad at me, Cade McMahon." She laughed as I handed her a red container of fries. "Eat your fries and be quiet," she ordered.

"Be quiet so you can get back to your murderous fantasy man?" I took my card back from the guy at the window and chomped on one of my fries as I pulled away. "If that's the kind of man you're looking for—one who'll off people for you—it's no wonder you don't have a boyfriend."

"Who says I don't?" she said as she chewed. "I never told you that."

"Deek said you were single."

"For someone who doesn't want anything to do with me, you *sure* seem interested in my business, Cade."

"I was merely curious whether there was a man out there who would put up with you." I winked. "So I inquired."

She searched the brown paper bag. "Damn. They forgot the ketchup."

"Want me to go back and kill someone?"

"No need." She licked some salt off her finger, causing my dick to twitch.

Yes, my dirty little secret was that I was *quite* attracted to this she-devil. But I'd never admit it. Daria was gorgeous, though. Long, fire-engine red hair and bright green eyes. Tats all the way up her arms and curves for days. She drove me nuts, but her beauty couldn't be denied.

Three hours later, we finally arrived at the cabin, just in the nick of time. As we carried in our stuff, it really started coming down outside. The place was sick, though—a fireplace, huge living area, and everything was brand, spanking new.

"Wow. This is beautiful," Daria said as she wandered around.

"Yeah. There are worse places to be stuck in a storm. That's for damn sure. Billie wasn't kidding."

She checked her phone. "Speaking of our boss, I wonder what time they're all supposed to get here. I don't know if we're supposed to start this party without them or what."

"Let me call and see how far away they are." I took my phone out and dialed Billie.

"Yes, Cade..." she answered.

"Hey! Where are you all? We just got here."

"Oh good, you made it."

"We did. How far away are you?"

"I'm in New York, actually. Sitting in my living room cuddling my kids. And Deek and Justine are still in New York, too."

"Um...why?" I scratched my head. "You should be at least halfway here by now."

"Well, you see, there's been a change of plans."

"What are you talking about?"

"We're not coming."

"What?" My eyes widened. "Why?"

"Because you two need to figure out your shit, and you don't need us there to do it."

A rush of adrenaline hit me. "You set us up?"

"I wouldn't call it a setup. More like an opportunity."

The balls on her. I gritted my teeth. "If you weren't my boss…"

"You'd what?" she challenged.

"I'd fire your ass."

Billie cracked up.

Daria squinted and mouthed, "What's going on?"

"I arranged for someone to deliver food earlier in the day," Billie said. "So you have plenty of grub and a box full of games so you can get to know each other. Stay until the storm passes, and figure out how to get along."

"And if we don't?"

"Then don't come back to the shop."

Tugging my hair, I exhaled. "Damn, boss, you play a tough game."

"It's all out of love," she said before hanging up.

Daria crossed her arms and huffed. "What the hell is going on?"

I let out a long breath. "It's just us this weekend. They set us up. There was no retreat."

Her eyes went wide. "What?"

"This whole thing was orchestrated for you and me—so we can work out our issues."

"Or kill each other," she seethed.

"Now, now, I'm not like your book characters," I teased.

"Seriously, Cade? This isn't a joke?"

"Unfortunately, it's not."

"What's the weather say? Is there any chance we can make it back?"

I pulled up the forecast on my phone. It looked like the heaviest bands of snow were coming straight at us in the next hour. "No, this says we're pretty much fucked." I pointed out the window. "You can see it's really coming down now, too."

She looked around and sighed. "Well, we're stuck here, I guess." She walked over to the kitchen. "Let's see what there is to eat."

Daria opened the fridge. There was a tray of cold cuts and other prepared foods.

"At least they didn't leave us to starve," I said. "We wouldn't have had much time to buy food ourselves before it started getting bad."

We unwrapped the tray, pulled out the other food, and ate in silence for a while, noshing until we'd made enough of a dent in it for one meal. And thank God they hadn't forgotten the alcohol. I had a nice buzz going, which made everything more tolerable. Made Daria look pretty damn hot, too. Okay, who was I kidding? She *was* hot. But again, I'd never give her the satisfaction of knowing I felt that way.

"We should play one of these team-building games while we're nice and buzzed so it's not so miserable," I suggested.

"What did she send...puzzles?" Daria asked.

"Let's open the box and find out."

I located scissors and sliced open the top of the box Billie had given me to take with us. When I looked inside, I didn't even know what to say. These were *not* the kind of games I was expecting.

I scratched my chin. "Okay...well, um..."

"What?" Daria asked as she poured wine from across the room.

"So...Billie's a freak."

CHAPTER 3

Daria

"Let me see that." I grabbed the cardboard box from Cade's hands and lifted out the game on top. "Sex Stack? What the hell is this?" The front had a picture of a normal Jenga-type, wooden-puzzle game. But there were numbers on the pieces, and arrows pointed to a stack of cards pictured off to the side. I read what was printed. "Oh my God. When you remove a piece, you pull out the card with the corresponding number on it, and you have to perform the act listed."

I placed the game on the table and pulled out another. *Oral Fun.* The slogan underneath read *The Game of Eating Out While Staying In.* I dropped that one like a hot potato, without even reading it to Cade, and reached for the next.

"Talk, Flirt, Dare," I read. This one didn't have too much information on the box, but it sounded similar to Truth or Dare. *Get to know your partner better* was the slogan. That seemed innocent enough, but the last thing I wanted was to get to know Cade any better, so I added that to the discard pile and dusted off my hands. "Maybe there's a deck of cards around here."

Cade stood. "Why don't you take a look, and I'll make a trip to that shed outside to see if there's any firewood?"

"Okay."

Our overnight bags were still by the front door. Cade unzipped his and pulled out a pair of bright blue ski pants and a matching sweater. The weirdo piled them on top of what he was already wearing, and then added a coat and boots. He looked ready to trek across Antarctica, not just fifty feet in the snow.

I arched a brow. "You sure you're going to be warm enough?"

He started to answer but then saw the look on my face. His eyes narrowed. "Pipe down, Red."

While Cade braved the frozen tundra, I searched the cabin for cards. Unfortunately, while the kitchen was nicely stocked, there wasn't any entertainment to be found. And I mean *none*. Not even a TV or stereo. But that turned out to be the least of our problems. Upstairs, I'd expected to find a few bedrooms, but there was only one. One bedroom. *One bed.*

When I came back down, Cade was shaking snow off at the front door, and there was a large pile of wood at his feet.

"We have a problem. There's only *one* bed in this house," I told him.

Cade shrugged. "So? You can sleep on the floor."

"*Me?* I'm not sleeping on the floor."

He unzipped his jacket and hung it on a hook. "Relax, Daria. I was joking. Not even *I'm* that big of a dick." He motioned to the couch. "I'll sleep there. You can have the bed."

"Oh. Okay. Thanks."

He finished peeling off his layers. "Did you find a deck of cards?"

I shook my head. "Nope. There isn't even a television."

"Billie said her in-laws bought the cabin recently and just finished renovating it. They probably didn't stock it with extras yet. I guess we should be glad there's a full shed of wood. I even found a box of fire starters."

I sighed. "What are we going to do all day? It's barely one o'clock since Billie made us leave at such an ungodly hour this morning. And the weather app says the snow is only going to get worse tonight. Even if it lets up early tomorrow, they'll still have to plow the roads. We're stuck here for at least twenty-four hours."

"I guess we'll both have to listen to your dark romance. You can put it on speaker."

"I am *not* listening to my book with you!"

"Why not?" He grinned. "Afraid I'll get some ideas and murder you?"

I wasn't about to share that my book had explicit sex scenes—ones that involved a dom with a filthy mouth and a sub with a praise kink. No way in hell was I going to listen to *that* with him. I'd rather walk home naked in this blizzard.

I shook my head. "I'm gonna put my phone on the charger and go upstairs and take a nice, hot bath. At least there's a big tub."

Cade was already loading wood into the fireplace. "Whatever floats your boat, princess."

The tub turned out to have whirlpool jets, so I soaked for the better part of an hour. It really helped unknot the tension in my neck that driving in the snow had caused. I felt so relaxed that I started to think I might be able to make it through this sham of a retreat without killing Cade.

Though that thought quickly disappeared the moment I walked down the stairs.

...and found Cade listening to my audiobook. I froze.

"That's a good girl," the male narrator's husky voice said. "Now get on your knees. You're going to take my cock down your throat until you can barely breathe. Do you hear me, Pet?"

"Yes, sir. I can't wait."

I blinked myself out of my stupor and took the last of the stairs two at a time, lunging for the man sitting on the couch when I hit the bottom. *"Give me that!"*

"Holy shit, Red. You like some fucked-up shit. But damn, this is *hot*."

I yanked my phone from his hand and stumbled, finding the button to turn off the volume. "You had no right to touch my phone!"

"Relax. I didn't do it on purpose. Billie called to make sure we hadn't killed each other yet. The storm must be affecting my cell service. She could hear me, but I couldn't make out what she was saying. So I told her to try calling back on your phone. I answered it on speaker. After she hung up, that audiobook automatically started to play. I didn't touch a thing to make it happen."

Shit. I did have a bad habit of forgetting to turn the audio off. Something similar had happened once on the subway. As the doors slid closed, I hung up with my sister on speakerphone and my book started playing—in the middle of a sex scene. Everyone around me stared, and I had to jump off at the next stop. "Yeah, well...it doesn't mean you had to listen. You should have turned it off as soon as you realized."

"The dude was spanking the woman with a paddle when it started. I'm a man—there's no way I was going to walk away from that."

I marched to the kitchen. "I need a drink."

"And I need a cigarette." Cade chuckled.

"Not funny."

"I thought it was."

I poured wine to the brim of my glass and started for the stairs. Thinking ahead, I stopped and marched back to the kitchen table, grabbing the open bottle. "I'm taking this with me."

"Enjoy your book, *Pet*."

I flipped him the bird. "Bite me, you jerk."

Cade's smirk widened. "I'm sure you're into that, too, sweetheart."

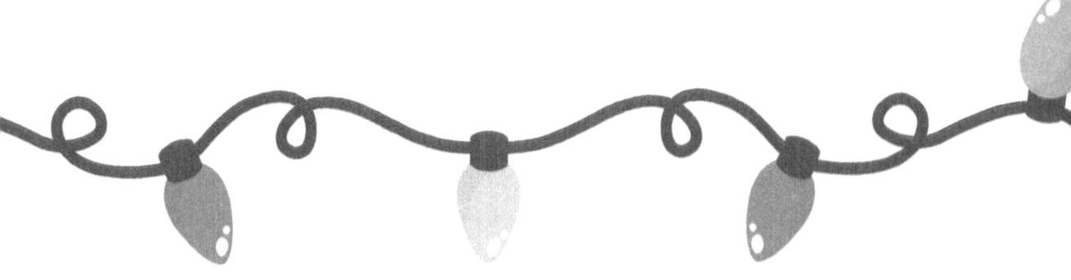

CHAPTER 4

Daria

After leaving me alone for about half an hour, Cade approached, speaking from outside the bedroom door.

"So...funny story..." he began.

I leaned up against the headboard. "What?"

"I texted Billie, like, 'What the fuck was up with those games?' And apparently, she didn't mean to send that box. She told her husband to order legitimate team-building games for us. Those are still in another box at their apartment. These games were meant for some romantic getaway they're gonna take. They gave us the wrong freaking box!"

"Oh my God." I laughed.

"Anyway, she told us to make the best of it," he said.

"How nice of her..."

"And how exactly do we do that?"

"We're supposed to work through our issues. If you stay in your room diddling yourself to your book the entire time, we're not gonna be able to tell Billie we made any progress."

I hopped up from the bed. "I'm not diddling, jackass. I'm avoiding you."

"Seriously, Daria. Why don't you come downstairs, and maybe we can figure out how to modify one of these games so they're not basically porn. Talk, Flirt, Dare doesn't look that bad."

"Or we could say we tried and not do anything." I leaned against the door.

"Billie's smarter than that. She's gonna ask what we did, and we're gonna have to get our stories straight. Might be easier to put the effort in and not have to bullshit her."

I sighed. "I guess you're right. If we can't prove we're getting along at least a little better, both our asses are on the line."

"I'm glad you agree."

I opened the door. "I'm gonna need more wine."

"On it." He winked as he ran ahead of me down the stairs.

Cade opened a fresh bottle of red, pouring us each a glass. He placed the board game on the coffee table, and we situated ourselves on the floor.

He took some time to read the instructions inside the box. "This game is pretty simple. You draw a question card, then ask the other person that question. They can either answer it, flirt with you, or submit to a dare. But the dares are written on cards they draw. So you don't tell them what to do. It's random." He tossed the instructions. "It says you can only choose flirt three times per person. The rest have to be answers to questions or dares."

Secretly a bit nervous to play, I exhaled. "What a stupid game."

"Right!" He took a drink of wine. "I mean, why play this game when you can be upstairs imagining being Dante's little pet?"

"I'm not listening to that book anymore." I grabbed a corn chip. "You ruined it for me."

Cade rubbed his hands together. "You want to draw a card first, or shall I?"

I shrugged. "I guess I will..." I reached for a card and previewed the question, smirking over at him. "Have you ever made a sex tape?"

"Oh." He scratched his chin scruff. "I'd have to think about that."

"What's there to think about? You either have or haven't."

"Yeah, but if I answer, I don't get to do a dare."

"Why would anyone want to be dared?" I tossed the card at him. "Just answer the damn question and put yourself out of your misery! Not like it matters one way or the other if you have a sex tape."

"That takes the fun out of the game." He paused. "Okay...dare." He reached over to the dare card stack and drew one. He read it silently and chuckled to himself.

"Read it," I said.

"Stare into your opponent's eyes and say something dirty without laughing." He started to crack up. "Fuck."

Oh boy.

He kept trying to put on a straight face, but ended up laughing over and over again. I was laughing now, too—laughing at what a goof he was.

Then he cleared his throat, long and hard. He seemed to get his shit together. Cade's expression turned serious. *Very* serious. His dark brown eyes seared into mine for several seconds, and you could hear a pin drop. Then, in a low, deep voice, he said, "I would *love* to fuck the hate you have for me right out of you, Red. Right up against that wall, right now—fuck you over and over until you're screaming my name and begging me not to stop."

A chill ran down my spine. That low, gravelly tone made my legs quiver. He could've given the guy who narrated my audiobook a run for his money.

I swallowed, trying not to seem affected. "Okay, nicely done. Moving on."

He set the dare card down, his face a tad red. "I guess it wasn't dirty enough, because I didn't offer to slice some guy's fingers off if he touched you, huh?"

I wouldn't be admitting that it was plenty dirty and had awakened something inside of me that I didn't want awakened—not by Cade McMahon, at least. *But damn.*

"Okay, my turn to ask you a question now," he said, reaching for a card. He snickered.

I lifted a brow. "What?"

"You're gonna *hate* this," he said, running a hand through his black hair.

"Not sure I can hate this game much more." I took a gulp of my wine. "So try me."

His eyes filled with mirth. "How many people have you slept with?"

My jaw dropped. "None of your damn business! They have some nerve asking that question in a stupid game."

"Welp." He shrugged. "Your choice. Looks like it's flirt or dare."

"No way I'm flirting with your ass, so I guess it's dare."

"Okay." He pointed to the pile of cards. "Draw your dare card, then."

I took the top one off the pile and read it.

I froze. *Oh, hell no.*

I slapped the card down on the table. "I need another one."

"Um..." He waved his index finger back and forth at me. "That's not how this game is played."

I crossed my arms. "Well, I'm sorry. I can't do this one."

"What the hell is so bad?" He grabbed the card and looked at it.

Take off either your shirt or pants.

CHAPTER 5

Cade

Iwouldn't have minded seeing some skin.

Especially after the way her green eyes had darkened to gray when I'd told her I wanted to fuck her. She'd felt me, whether she'd ever admit it or not. But as much as I'd enjoy seeing what was underneath the funky clothes she wore, I wouldn't do that to Daria. Not to any woman. If a woman wanted to take her clothes off for me, it would be her choice. Not some game.

"New rule," I said.

"You can't make up new rules."

"Show me the rule that says I can't make up new rules."

Daria rolled her eyes. "What are you proposing?"

"Each player gets two steals."

"What does that mean?"

"It means at any time during the game, either of us can decide to take the other player's card and use it as our turn." I leaned forward and plucked the one currently in her hand.

"Are you serious? You *want* to take your clothes off?"

I shrugged. "I got nothing to hide."

Daria nibbled her lip. She probably suspected I was trying to let her off the hook and was debating what was worse—accepting my help or getting naked in front of me. Eventually she sighed. "Fine. I accept your rule modification."

It wouldn't be as much fun, that was for damn sure, but I worked hard on my body and never minded showing it off. Though, if I was stripping, I sure as hell was going to make it an act she'd remember. I dug my cell out of my pocket, opened the Spotify app, and searched up some Marvin Gaye. Scrolling until I found the perfect song, I hit speaker and stood as "Sexual Healing" began.

Daria watched me like I needed my head examined. But her face changed as I lifted the hem of my shirt and teased taking it off while gyrating my hips. My good-for-nothing father hadn't given me much, but he did give me rhythm and hips that swiveled better than Elvis. *Magic Mike's got nothing on me.*

I put on a show worthy of big bills at the strip club, and Daria's jaw hung open while she watched. Once I'd finally removed my shirt, she swallowed. It took a solid thirty seconds before she blinked out of her haze.

"Well, I guess we know what you did before becoming a tattoo artist," she said.

"My ex-roommate was a stripper. He might've showed me some moves." I sat back down without my shirt. Daria's eyes wandered to my abs twice more before she looked away. "You can get dressed now, Moron Mike."

I could've busted her balls about the look she'd had on her face while watching me, but for some reason, I didn't. Daria grabbed the next Talk card from the pile and scanned it before sighing.

"What's it say?"

"Tell the player across from you what you find most attractive about them."

I smiled from ear to ear and leaned back to clasp my hands behind my head. "That's got to be a hard one, since everything about me is so attractive."

Daria rolled her eyes. "If only your personality matched the packaging."

"Did you just say you think I'm *hot*, Red?"

She shook her head. "It figures you took *that* from my statement and not the fact that your personality is shitty."

I ignored her. "So let's hear it. What part of my body turns you on the most?"

Clearly it pained her to have to compliment me. Which I very much enjoyed.

Daria tossed the card with a sigh. "Fine. Your chest doesn't look *that* bad." She shook her head and climbed up off the floor. "I need more wine."

While she refilled her glass, I cheated a little. I took the card she'd just discarded and put it back on the top of the Talk pile, leaving a different one in its place. She came back a minute later, none the wiser.

"Your turn."

I tapped my finger to my lip. "Hmm... I think I'll take a Talk card this time around."

Picking up the top card, I pretended to read it. "Tell the player across from you what you find most attractive about them."

"Seriously?" She glanced at what she thought was the card she'd discarded on the floor, but didn't pick it up. "Two of the same card? We should have shuffled better. What if I'd picked that one up too?"

I shrugged. "Guess you would've had to tell me *another* thing you find attractive about me. That would've been easy, obviously."

Daria sipped her wine. "Fine. Go ahead. Make a crass comment about my ass or tits and get it over with."

I'd rigged the game to do exactly that, but when my eyes snagged on her lips, my brain called an audible. "Your lips," I said.

"Really? That's so...clean."

I smirked. "Not if I tell you what I could stick between them."

"Pig."

I laughed. "Seriously though, you have a great smile." I pointed to the middle of her top lip. "The top of your mouth forms a little bow. And when you smile—really smile, not evil smile like you usually do around me—it feels like that bow is on top of a present."

Daria blinked. "Oh my God. That's so sweet."

"I have my moments."

She squinted. "You're not trying to sweet talk me to get in my pants, are you? Because even though I'm already a little tipsy, that is *definitely* not going to happen."

I shook my head. "Just pick a card, she-devil."

"She-devil? That's a new one."

"Not really. I call you that in my head all the time."

For the next few hours, Daria and I played the game. We also finished off the second bottle of wine, which was probably why I'd become so loose with my answers. Alcohol was like truth serum for me. But we laughed a lot and were having a pretty good time. Daria had just finished a dare where she had to fake an orgasm. She was definitely drunk now because she'd hiccupped in the middle of it, which made us both roll on the floor in hysterics.

"Your turn." *Hiccup.* She covered her mouth. "Damn, these things won't go away. You might have to scare me."

I picked up a card from the Dare pile this time, figuring I'd wait until she least expected it before I tried to scare away her hiccups. Though once I read the card in my hand, I was the one scared.

Text your ex that you miss them.

CHAPTER 6

Daria

"**R**ead it," I chided as Cade continued to hold the dare card and not say anything.

What the hell is wrong with him? All of a sudden, he's timid about this game?

"I..." He swallowed.

"What?"

He shook his head. "I can't do this one."

"I thought we were supposed to be playing by the rules!"

His face reddened. "Yeah, but—"

"Let me see." I whipped the card out of his grasp before he could react. *Text your ex that you miss them. Hmm...* "Okay..." I looked up at him. "So, this one is definitely awkward, but I didn't take you for the embarrassed-easily type." I examined his face. "Unless you fucked up *so* badly with your ex that you're too ashamed to text her? Exactly what did you do?"

"Nothing, and I don't have an ex," he muttered.

"Well, now I'm *really* confused. You don't have an

ex." I crossed my arms. "So then what's the problem? Incidentally, I'm not buying that. *Everyone* has an ex."

"I've only had one serious relationship."

"She's not your current girlfriend?"

"No."

"Then she's your *ex*."

"Can we please drop it?" His expression was sincere, his eyes pleading.

Whatever had happened between Cade and his ex, it was apparently tearing him up inside right now. Though I was quite tempted to prod some more, something told me not to push.

"You know what?" I slammed the card on the table. "I'm about to prove once and for all that I have bigger balls than you."

"How?"

I leaned in and said, "Steal."

His eyes widened. "You're gonna steal this dare from me?"

"Well, you made that stupid rule. This is my first of two steal allowances." I smiled. "And believe me, texting my ex is just about the most mortifying thing I could be doing right now."

Cade arched a brow. "Why is that?"

"Because he's getting married to my friend."

"What?"

"It gets worse." I sighed, feeling my cheeks burn. "The wedding...is on Christmas Eve."

"That's in a few days," he pointed out.

"Yep." I chuckled. "It gets *even* worse."

"Damn. How?"

"I was *invited* to the wedding."

"They had the nerve to invite you?"

"Yeah, and I had the nerve to accept!"

His eyes nearly bugged out of his head. "You're going?"

"They're both under the delusion that I'm fine with it. Truth be told, he and I were broken up when he started seeing her. But I was still in love with him. And it still fucking hurts."

"Damn." Cade frowned. "I'm sorry, Daria. I don't know who to despise more—him or this woman who was supposed to be your friend."

"It is what it is."

"Don't text that asshole on my account."

I hiccupped. "I think it might be fun, actually. Ruffle his feathers a little before the wedding."

"Well, I'm not gonna stop you." He laughed. "Heck, I'll go pop the fucking popcorn."

"No time for popcorn." I grinned as I took out my phone. "This is happening."

Cade leaned over my shoulder. The nearness of his body and his musky scent were not lost on me as I typed.

I miss you.

The little dots started moving.

Derek: Are you drunk?

Our shoulders shook with laughter.

"Touché, dickwad," Cade said.

Daria: Maybe.

Derek: Then I'm gonna assume you don't mean what you just said.

"Let's mess with him." Cade spoke into my ear.

Daria: What if I do mean it?

Derek: Then that would be pretty inappropriate.

Cade took the phone before I could stop him and started to type.

Daria: Inappropriate is you getting married to my supposed friend. But what do I know?

Shit! I turned to him. "Good one."

Derek: Are you serious? I thought you were over that.

I took the phone from Cade and typed.

Daria: Actually, this whole message was a dare. I have balls bigger than Cade, so I stole it. Have a good day.

Derek: Huh? Balls? You're not making sense. Who's Cade?

"Can I?" Cade pleaded as he held his hand out.
I passed him the phone. "Go for it."
Cade typed.

Daria: Cade is someone with balls bigger than YOU and a WAY bigger dick.

I covered my mouth in laughter, which was interrupted by another hiccup, as one final text came in from Derek.

Derek: Take care of yourself. Don't drive.

"Take care of yourself?" Cade tossed the phone. "What a douche."

"He's so out of touch, even if he thinks I'm drunk off my ass right now. He doesn't realize the magnitude of what he did to me. He believes it was okay because we were broken up."

"He could've dated literally any other woman in the world. But instead, he decided to date your friend? *Marry* her? That takes a special kind of asshole." He turned to me. "What's her name?"

"Sharon."

"Sharon. *Another* asshole."

"Thank you!" I smiled. "That felt good."

"But okay...we need to discuss this." He placed his hand on my shoulder, causing my body to buzz. "Why the hell are you going to the wedding?"

That was the question. I had a few answers, and I hoped he understood where I was coming from. Cade's opinion suddenly mattered to me, either because of my drunkenness or something more. Perhaps I'd learned to trust him in the course of this fucked-up afternoon.

"A few reasons..." I hiccupped. "One, declining the invitation would've made it look like I still have feelings for him. And while I have *hard* feelings toward him, I could never love someone who would do what he did. So any love I had for him is in the past. This is more about me showing them I've moved on. Two, they're getting married at The Ritz, and it's an open bar. The food should be good, too. So why the hell not? Three, I have a killer dress that's cut all the way down to my navel in the front. Derek's brother is a boob man and single."

Cade snapped his fingers. "Ah…revenge!"

"I'm sort of joking about that. Two wrongs don't make a right."

"Fuck that! You'd be totally in the right to date his brother."

"His brother's a tool, though," I noted.

"Okay, so maybe not." Cade winked. "But yeah, the killer dress sounds nice."

"It is." I grinned mischievously. "Can I ask you a question outside of this game?"

"Yeah."

"What happened with your ex? What had you all worked up about that dare?"

He looked up at the ceiling before meeting my eyes again. "She died."

And just like that, my hiccups were gone.

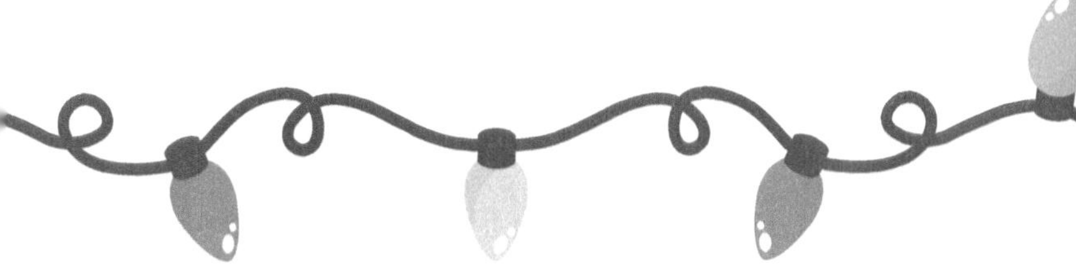

CHAPTER 7

Cade

"Oh shit." I grimaced. "Are you crying?"

"No." Daria turned away.

I reached out and cupped her chin, turning her to face me. Fat tears streamed down her cheeks. I couldn't help but crack a smile. "You're not crying, huh?"

"Shut up, jerk. I got something in my eye."

I'd never thought it would be possible to laugh while talking about Everly's death, but somehow Daria had done it. I chuckled. "Must be a bucket of water you got in there."

She sniffled and swiped at her cheeks. "I'm so sorry, Cade. I shouldn't have pushed you on the subject. I...I just didn't think..."

"It's okay. It was two years ago. She died in a car accident. A resident doctor who had just worked a twenty-four-hour shift fell asleep at the wheel on his way home. His car swerved into oncoming traffic, and he hit her head on. He didn't make it either."

"Oh, God. That's horrible." Daria kept shaking her head. "I'm so sorry."

"Thank you." I fell silent. But for a change, it wasn't because I was brooding over Everly—though talking about her would always leave a hollow feeling in my chest. This time I was debating coming clean about one of the reasons Daria had irked me from the first moment we'd met. She'd been honest about her asshole ex, so I figured I owed her some truth. Plus, I was pretty buzzed. "Everly might have something to do with the reason I've been a dick to you."

Daria used the backs of her hands to dry her cheeks. "I don't understand."

"I don't dream every night. Well, at least I don't remember it, if I do. But a few times a year, I wake up after a really vivid dream. For more than eighteen months after Everly died, the dreams were always about her. Sometimes it would be a memory. I'd dream about something we did together. Other times it would be random shit my brain made up—like I'd be sitting in a movie theater watching a movie and she'd be the actress in it, even though she wasn't an actress. But that changed when I met you."

"You stopped dreaming about her?"

I swallowed and looked into Daria's eyes. "I started dreaming about *you*."

Her jaw dropped open.

I nodded. "Yeah. I had a lot of guilt about that. So I might've taken it out on you."

"What were the dreams about?"

"Usually we were arguing."

She smiled. "Shocker."

"But then we'd wind up...you know."

Daria's eyes widened. "Cade McMahon, are you saying you had *dirty dreams* about me?"

I frowned. I wasn't proud of it. "I had to shut you the hell up somehow."

Daria was quiet for a long time. Eventually, she picked up her half-full glass of wine and chugged it back in one long gulp. "Hopefully I won't remember I admitted this tomorrow," she said. "But here goes... I sometimes use you as my fantasy when I...you know."

It was my turn to be shocked as shit. "Are you saying you masturbate to thoughts of me?"

She buried her face in her hands. "I can't believe I told you that."

This conversation had taken a turn, one that had me growing hard as fuck. It was totally inappropriate, but I couldn't help it. The thought of her touching herself while thinking of me, rubbing her fingers over her glistening clit, pushing them inside while moaning my name. *Fuck. Me.* I dragged a hand through my hair. "That's fucking hot, Daria."

"What the hell is wrong with us?" she asked. "We spew venom at each other all day at work, and then go home and do that?"

"I don't know. I guess sometimes all that pent-up anger spills out in ways you don't expect. Especially when the other person is freaking gorgeous."

Daria gasped. "You think I'm attractive?"

"We work in a shop with a wall of mirrors, Red. That can't come as a surprise to you."

She looked down, shaking her head. "I used to like my appearance, but I think Derek made me doubt myself."

"Because he got with your friend?"

"That and...I'm pretty sure he was embarrassed of me."

Anger coursed through my veins. "What the fuck? Why would he be embarrassed of you?"

"He's an attorney at some snobby law firm where everyone graduated from Columbia, Yale, or Harvard. When we first started dating, he seemed attracted to me. But whenever we'd go to one of his work functions, he'd tell me to wear long sleeves." She sighed. "My friend Sharon, who he's marrying next week, doesn't have any tattoos or piercings. I think she has cashmere sweater sets in every color. She's really pretty."

"Sharon sounds like a boring mouse he'll be cheating on by their first anniversary."

Daria smiled sadly. "Thank you for saying that."

"I'm not just saying it to make you feel good, Daria. I'm being honest. You're fucking gorgeous—from the top of your head to the tips of your toes. Your body is killer, and your face looks like an angel. Then you add all that sexy-as-fuck ink on top, and you're like every man's wet dream."

"Except Derek, apparently."

"Fuck Derek! He's a moron. Any man who tells his woman to cover her ink because she might not fit in with his suit-wearing coworkers isn't a man at all. He's an insecure follower."

Daria still didn't look like she was getting it. So I slipped two fingers under her chin and lifted until our eyes met. "The problem in your last relationship wasn't you, sweetheart. It was him. Any man would be lucky to have you."

Her eyes roamed over my face. Then she did the last thing in the world I expected. She smashed her lips to mine...

CHAPTER 8

Daria

Holy shit, his lip ring felt good against my tongue. And his tongue felt even better against my tongue—I knew it would feel amazing against other places, too. Kissing Cade was better than I could have dreamed. It was the best kiss of my life, in fact.

The forceful way he held my face almost immediately after I planted one on him? Epic. Despite me making the first move, Cade quickly transformed into the aggressor. And I was here for it.

Everything about the way he kissed was perfection—the rhythm of his tongue, the subtle groans coming from deep in the back of his throat. I was wetter by the second, especially with the heat of his massive package pressed against my abdomen.

"Damn, Cade." I moaned into his mouth. "What are you doing to me right now? You're making me crazy."

When he spoke, low against my lips, my panties nearly melted off. "You have no idea how badly I want to fuck you right now, Daria."

"Spoiler alert…" I threaded my fingers through his hair. "I'll let you."

"Shit." Panting, he pulled back. "I can't." He shook his head. "God, do I want to, but I can't."

I licked the remnants of his kiss off my bottom lip—it suddenly tasted like rejection. And it stung. I cleared my throat. "You can't…"

He wrapped his big tatted hand gently around my neck. "You're a little drunk. Actually, *quite* drunk. I would never know if you truly wanted it. You need to be sober."

Bending my head back, I closed my eyes as he began to massage the back of my neck. "I promise you, I want it." I *did* want him, so badly that my nipples were practically begging me for mercy.

But he had a point. We'd both had too much to drink. And his not taking advantage of the situation proved what a decent guy he really was.

Cade's eyes were hazy. "I can't take the chance that you'd feel differently tomorrow. I don't want you to have any regrets." He pointed down at his crotch. "Believe me, it's not that I don't want it. Fucking look at this thing. I couldn't get any harder for you if I tried."

My mouth practically watered as I took him in. But if nothing was going to happen between us, it was better if I separated myself from the bulge in his jeans—and cooled down.

"You know what?" I ran a hand down the length of my hair. "I should probably head to my room. We can clean up this mess tomorrow."

Before he could say anything more, I left him there with a hard-on as I practically ran up the stairs. *What the hell has gotten into you, Daria?*

Well, I knew what *hadn't* gotten into me in apparently too long a while.

I sighed.

After tossing off my shoes, I climbed into bed. I couldn't stop thinking about Cade. We'd been stuck in this cabin not even a day together, but something had shifted. It was weird. I didn't know what all this meant—it had happened so fast. After the storm cleared and we left here, would we go back to the way things were? Was our connection exclusive to being trapped in this cabin—or was it something more? The prospect of something more with the last guy on Earth I'd ever expected to connect with scared me as much as it excited me. *We work together!* What if we screwed things up, and one of us had to quit? We both loved working at the shop so much.

I was getting ahead of myself and needed to stop ruminating. But I couldn't help it.

I really like him.

I knew one thing: I would *not* be throwing myself at him tomorrow when this sex fog cleared. I definitely needed to backtrack there.

Later that evening, after a lot of scrolling through my phone, I had just about dozed off when I heard the door creak open. A couple seconds later, the bed sank as I felt Cade's weight on the mattress. That was followed by the warmth of his body at my back.

"Are you awake?" he whispered gruffly.

I stayed frozen and said nothing. It was just easier to pretend to be asleep.

"Well, isn't that great." He chuckled. "You're asleep, and I'm wired."

With my back still turned to him, I smiled.

He went on. "I'm gonna have to assume that since you apparently wouldn't have minded if I stuck my dick inside you tonight, you won't mind if I sleep next to you. I really don't feel like sleeping on the couch. But hopefully you won't kick me in the balls when you wake up and find me here."

My mouth curved into another smile, which soon faded when he changed the subject.

"I can't believe I told you about Everly. But I guess I had no choice. I didn't want to lie." He exhaled. "I never talk about her. It's too damn painful. Especially around this time of year." He paused. "She died close to Christmas…"

I shut my eyes tightly to fight the tears.

"It's part of why I hate the holidays so much." He blew out a breath. "Anyway, you make it easy to open up, Red. Even when we're fighting at work, I don't hold back with you. You give me this…boost of energy that I don't experience with anyone else. I like fighting with you more than most things. That's probably why I dream of you." He sighed deeply. "You're…fire. Gorgeous fire. And I hope you don't turn me down when I take my shot again sometime when we're both sober."

Now I really wanted to turn around and plant another kiss on his luscious lips. But instead, I replayed his words in my head and listened to the sound of his breathing as we both drifted off to sleep.

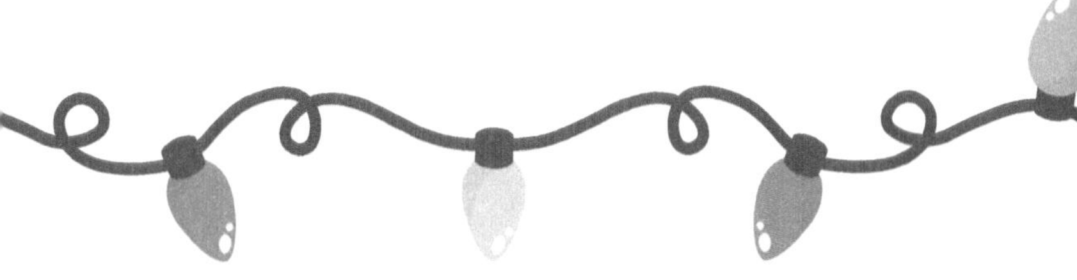

CHAPTER 9

Cade

I woke to an empty bed.

A ray of sun streaked in through the window, cutting a rude path directly across my eyes. I threw my arm over my face and groaned.

What time is it?

And where the hell is Daria?

The house was quiet, not a peep to be heard.

Fuck. Did she leave without me?

I whipped the covers off and sprang out of bed, taking the stairs two at a time in a panic. When I got to the bottom, I found Daria staring out the kitchen window, her hands wrapped around a mug.

"Everything okay?" I asked.

She jumped. "Shit. I didn't hear you come down."

"Sorry." I raked a hand through my hair. "How long have you been up?"

"I don't know. Maybe an hour."

"What time is it?"

"About seven, I guess."

The smell of coffee wafted through the air. An almost-full glass pot sat on the counter, so I helped myself. Daria stayed put, not saying a word. Once I fixed my coffee, I walked over and stood beside her as she continued to gaze out the window.

Yesterday's blizzard had turned into today's winter wonderland. Tree branches bowed under the weight of heavy white powder, icicles glistened from eaves, and the ground sparkled with a pristine canvas of snow.

"Wow," I said. "I've wanted to paint the world with color since I picked up my first can of spray paint at ten years old. But some things are art without trying. Goddamn, Mother Nature is a showoff."

Daria smiled. "Yeah."

We stood that way for a long time, just sipping our coffee and appreciating the beauty. Eventually Daria's cup was empty. "You want a refill?" I asked.

"I got it." She spoke as she poured. "I checked the weather. There's a break in the snow until tonight. The last of the flurries are supposed to taper off soon. But another heavy band is coming in around midnight. So if we want to get out of here, we should hit the road as soon as they're done plowing. Otherwise, we might get stuck here."

My eyes stayed locked on her. "I can think of worse places to be."

She smiled, but it was weak. Her face didn't join in on the action. "Listen, Cade. About last night... I need to apologize."

"For what?"

"I had too much to drink, and I shouldn't have kissed you."

"Why not?"

"Oh, I don't know. Because we work together. Because we don't even like each other. Because you were drinking.

Because I was drinking. Because we are at our boss's in-laws' house, where we're supposed to be working our shit out, not making things more complicated." She shook her head. "Do I need to keep going?"

"I wasn't that drunk."

Daria sighed. "Do you think we can forget it ever happened?"

Considering it was the best kiss of my life, I doubted it would be erased from my memory anytime soon. But if that's how she wanted to handle things, I wasn't going to be a dick. I shrugged. "Sure."

The worry lines in her forehead smoothed out. "Could we also keep what happened between us? I'd rather not have everyone at work know I drunk-mauled you."

"Of course. But for the record, I kissed you back. You weren't the only one doing the mauling."

She held out a hand hesitantly. "What happens at the ski cabin, stays at the ski cabin?"

"Whatever you want."

For the next couple of hours, we pretty much kept our distance. I went outside, shoveled a path, and dug the car out, while Daria cleaned up everything inside the house. Once the plows came by and cleared the street, and the weather report said the main roads were passable, we decided it was time to go.

Daria stood in the living room, looking around. "So did Billie's evil plan work? Do you think we'll be able to keep our truce once we're back at the shop?"

"I don't know. I kinda like fighting with you."

She smiled. "Maybe we can go a round every once in a while, for old times' sake."

"Sounds good. Though I should probably let you in on a little secret about our fights."

"Oh? What's that?"

I lowered my voice and leaned over to her. "They turn me the fuck on."

Goosebumps ran up Daria's arms, and she bit her bottom lip. "Same."

I groaned. "Sounds like work might be a lot more fun from now on."

Our differences settled, it felt like time to go. Yet neither of us made a move for the door. I knew it was stupid, considering Daria wanted to pretend last night had never happened, but part of me wasn't ready to burst the bubble we'd been in. I liked it here. It felt warm and fuzzy. I liked the Daria who opened up to me, and I was glad I'd let her in, too. I felt closer to her now. Though I knew in my gut that once we walked out the door, things were going to change. Sure, some of it would be for the better—we probably wouldn't brawl at work all day long, and our boss wouldn't be close to firing us—but maybe I wanted more from Daria. More getting to know her. More laughing together. More of that kiss...

Daria sighed. "You ready to go?"

"Sure."

We walked to the door. But the minute I opened it, panic washed over me. *What if this is all I get with her?* I pushed the door back shut.

"What are you doing? Did you forget something?"

"What happens at the cabin, stays at the cabin, right?"

"Yeah."

"Then there's one more thing I need to do before we go."

"What?"

I cupped the back of her neck and pulled her to me. "This..."

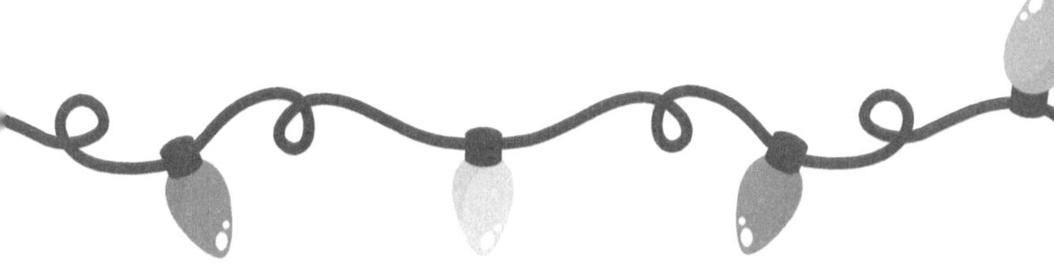

CHAPTER 10

Daria

"Where are you going dressed like that?" Billie asked. She was locking the shop up early for the holiday.

I'd gone to the back room to change into my dress since I wouldn't have time to go all the way home and make it to the church on time.

I looked down at myself. "You don't like it?"

"Are you kidding? You look hot!"

"I have to go to my ex's wedding straight from here."

Her eyes widened. "Well, that explains the dress." She shook her head. "But wait...a wedding on Christmas Eve? Who the hell plans a wedding on Christmas Eve?"

"Selfish, self-absorbed people."

"I was gonna say..." She sighed. "Hey, I've been meaning to ask, what went down at the cabin between you and Cade? You and he were kind of quiet this week. And it's been so busy, I haven't had a chance to talk to you."

Cade and I had exchanged many glances during our shifts together since returning from the retreat. But with the holiday rush, the shop was so busy. He and I had never had much chance to talk. My shifts ended before his, so he was always still working when I went home.

"The cabin was a good experience. We have a new respect for each other. Let's just say, your plan worked."

Billie chuckled. "What did you guys *do*, though? Obviously, we sent you with the wrong box of activities. I felt bad about that—even if it took me a while to stop laughing about it."

"Believe it or not, we were quite resourceful. We made the best of the truth-or-dare-like game and used it to get to know each other better." I shrugged. "The alcohol helped."

"Well, I'm proud of you guys for working things out." She laughed. "I'm glad I don't have to fire either one of you, because you're two of the best talents I've ever had."

"Thanks." I smiled. "Do you happen to know why Cade called out today? I thought he was on the schedule."

"I don't know. He just said something came up. He only had one client booked, and I'm not gonna get pissy at him on Christmas Eve."

"Okay," I muttered. I just hoped he wasn't avoiding me now that we were back to reality. Was he thinking better of that last amazing kiss we'd shared before we left Vermont? I couldn't stop thinking about it. I shook my head, needing to snap out of it and not analyze why he was out today. It was Christmas Eve, and the shop had closed early anyway. Cade probably took the day off to see family. Or maybe he had to travel somewhere.

"Anyway, I hope you have an amazing Christmas, Billie," I said as I approached the door to leave.

"You too! Colby and I are hosting friends tonight. Try to have a good time at the wedding—or at the very least, give your ex hell in that dress."

As I stepped out into the cold air, I decided to walk a

couple of blocks before calling a car. I had a little time to kill and wanted to savor the feel of Christmas in the air as last-minute shoppers whizzed by me on the streets.

But with every step I took, I doubted more and more why I was even bothering with this wedding tonight. For some reason, I'd felt differently about attending since my time with Cade at the cabin. His surprise over the fact that I'd planned to go had made me question it myself. I didn't need to prove anything to anyone. It was Christmas Eve, and I'd be better off spending time with my family than with two people who had hurt me.

In that moment, my brain made an executive decision on behalf of my heart. Instead of calling a car to take me to the church, I hopped on the subway and went to my cousin's house, where I knew many of my family members would be getting together later. My family would probably give me shit for the sexy dress I was wearing on Christmas, but at least it was red, right?

Two-and-a-half hours later, I was standing by the punch bowl that was sitting on my cousin Maureen's red-linen-covered table when my phone chimed with a text.

Did you decide not to go to the wedding after all?

It had come from an unknown number. I texted back.

Daria: Who is this?

Cade: It's Cade. Billie gave me your number.

My heart came alive as I typed.

Daria: Oh! Hey! Yeah, actually, I didn't go. Listened to your advice. Decided they didn't deserve my presence. I'm at a family party.

Cade: Ah.

Daria: Wait…how did you know I decided not to go?

Cade: I'm at the reception and couldn't find you.

Oh my God.

Daria: What?

Cade: I wanted to see you, so I crashed the wedding. You told me where it was, remember? I was hoping to catch you.

Excitement filled me.

Daria: You're there now?

Cade: You were right about the food—the appetizers were awesome.

Adrenaline pumped through my veins.

Daria: Don't move. I'm coming.

Cade: You don't have to, if you have other plans.

Daria: No. I want to! Where will you be?

Cade: At the top of the staircase outside the ballroom.

I called out to my cousin, who I knew was a fast driver. "Bruno, I need a ride!"

The grand white staircase was adorned with gold accents, tinsel, and large red Christmas bulbs woven through the banister. I rushed up the stairs, and then I saw him. *Holy shit.* Cade wore a black suit and red satin tie. He was holding his jacket, and his sleeves were rolled up, showcasing his colorful ink. He looked beyond hot—holding a bouquet of roses.

He shook his head slowly when he spotted me. "Wow," he said, almost breathlessly. "You were right. That dress is killer." He handed me the flowers.

As we stood facing each other, there was so much I wanted to say. "I haven't been able to stop thinking about you, Cade," I blurted, barely aware of the wedding reception in the ballroom—I couldn't have cared less. "I was afraid the reason you called out today was because you'd thought better of everything that went down with us and were avoiding me."

"Are you kidding? The only regret I have is what *didn't* go down, if you know what I mean. I can't stop thinking about you, either. I just want to be back at that cabin. I know it's Christmas, and I'm supposed to be with my family—assembling my nephew's presents tonight or whatever—but I only want to be with you." He looked into my eyes. "I called out of work today because I had to wedding prep—grooming myself, picking up a suit that fit, and getting you flowers—hoping to crash this thing and find you."

My eyes began to water. "I'll never forget this." Then, I couldn't help myself. I leapt into his arms, and to my surprise, he lifted me. Wrapping my legs around his tall frame, I kissed him with everything I had, this time not caring at all whether I came across as too forward.

"Daria?"

Cade and I broke our kiss as we turned in unison. Derek stood there, dressed in his white wedding tux, looking shocked at the spectacle I'd just made.

As Cade put me down slowly, I wiped my lips. "Oh... hey, Derek. Didn't notice you there."

"I can see that." He looked up at Cade. "I didn't know you were bringing someone."

"I didn't bring him. He met me here...although, I just got here myself. In fact, we were just leaving." I took Cade's hand and stood proudly. "This is Cade."

"Ah." Derek nodded. "Mr. Big Dick himself. I wasn't sure if you were real, considering how drunk she was when she texted me the other day."

"That was actually *me* texting you about my dick. But yeah... I'm very real."

Derek squinted in confusion. The look on his face was priceless.

"He's real, Derek." I smiled up at Cade. "He's my man. Thank you so much for breaking up with me so I could find the real deal." I squeezed Cade's hand as I told Derek one last thing. "It all worked out the way it was supposed to. I *do* wish you and Sharon the best of luck. You're perfect for each other."

Cade lifted me again, carrying me away like a caveman as we made our theatrical exit down the grand staircase. I never looked back, though catching one more glimpse of Derek's flabbergasted expression might've been nice.

"I don't like the way he was staring at your tits just now," Cade growled in my ear.

"I didn't notice, but mighty possessive, aren't we?"

"Well, you called me your man. I don't want anyone staring at *my woman's* tits, except me."

I ran my fingers through his hair. "I think you have some anger issues. You might need to take some of that aggression out on me." I kissed his cheek. "Take it out on my totally clear-minded, *sober* ass, by the way."

He wriggled his brows. "Now you've got me thinking about that ass."

As we made it to the lobby, I asked, "Do you think they have rooms available?"

"Only one way to find out." He put me down.

Cade went to the front desk, spoke to the attendant, and flashed me two big thumbs up. When I tried to give him my wallet, he shooed me away. So I waited in the wings, taking deep inhales of the roses he'd bought me, wondering how what was slated to be one of the worst nights of my life had turned out to be the best.

A few minutes later, Cade returned, waving the key-card as he flashed me a devilish smile.

"Thanks, Santa." I winked.

We hopped into the elevator, and he backed me up against the wall and showered my neck with kisses. "This might be my favorite Christmas ever, beautiful. And it's just getting started."

I bent my neck back in ecstasy and exhaled. "Safe to say, Santa Claus is definitely *coming* to town tonight."

THE END

THE CHRISTMAS CARD

CHAPTER 1

Joy

"**W**hen are you going to put yourself out of your misery and stop coming to this stupid party?" My best friend Isla grabbed a second champagne flute from the tray of a passing waiter and chugged half of it back. "*Mmm...* At least your ex buys the good stuff."

Out of the corner of my eye, I spotted Davis. His fiancée, Hailey, was snuggled close. Seeing them together caused a pang of...*something* in my chest, though I wasn't sure what that *something* was anymore. I was long over my ex, for the most part. As I should be, considering it had been almost two years since we split up. But before that, I'd been the co-host of this annual Christmas party. Maybe what I felt was just jealousy—not so much about losing the man, but that Hailey didn't have to kiss any more frogs to find her prince. Dating in New York was the absolute pits.

"We all work together, and I don't want everyone at the office to think I'm still pining over Davis," I explained.

Isla rolled her eyes. "Who gives a shit what people think?"

I smiled and bumped shoulders with my friend. "Certainly not you."

Isla and I were complete opposites in that regard. I cared too much what others thought, and she cared too little. We both sipped champagne while looking over at Davis and his fiancée.

"He definitely has a type," she murmured.

More than one person had mentioned that Hailey looked like me, though I didn't see it—other than we both had chestnut hair and fair skin. Davis must've felt eyes on him, because he suddenly lifted his head from his conversation and looked over. He smiled and tilted his champagne flute in our direction.

I offered a genuine smile back. I didn't have any hard feelings toward him. Our breakup had been mostly my fault. Davis and I had been a couple for almost three years, and he'd started pushing me to move in with him and get engaged. At the time, I hadn't been sure I was ready. I now realized I had commitment issues, ones that had more to do with my dad cheating on my mom regularly and my high school boyfriend dying in a car accident than anything Davis had or hadn't done. I'd always been nervous about getting too attached to people. So when Davis pushed, I pushed back—telling him I needed time to make sure he was *the one* before taking that next big step. Three months later, I was ready. But the night I'd planned to tell Davis, he'd told me he'd met someone—Hailey, his now-fiancée. She had just started working at the company we both worked for.

"Come on, let's go over and say hello." Isla linked arms with me and started us walking. "Then we can get the hell out of here and have some real fun at Evie's Christmas party."

"Okay. But we have to stay and mingle for at least a half hour so no one from work asks me why I disappeared so fast."

Isla shook her head. "There you go again, caring about stupid shit."

We'd made it halfway across the room when two men walked in and snagged my attention. One was a friend of Davis's whom I vaguely recognized, but the taller guy was drop-dead gorgeous. Why did he look so familiar? I kept walking as I tried to place the face. When I did, I stopped in my tracks.

"Oh my God. *Oh my God*! Isla, we need to get out of here right now!"

"Why? What's the matter?"

"He's here! My fake boyfriend. He's here!"

"What in God's name are you talking about?"

"Do you remember the fake boyfriend I made up and told everyone at work about after Davis and I broke up? You know, because everyone kept coming up to me with sympathetic faces and asking if I was okay after Davis and Hailey got together?"

"Yeah, I remember. That's another time you cared too much about what other people think. You gave the fake boyfriend a name, too, right?"

"Nolan."

"Right. Nolan. But what do you mean he's here? I thought you made him up."

My heart pounded. "I used some random hot guy I came across online."

"So? What's the big deal?"

I closed my eyes. "This is so damn embarrassing. That's why I never told you. But I did more than just tell my coworkers I was dating someone. Last December, I got a holiday card in the mail from Davis. It was also an engagement announcement. It had a picture of the happy couple standing under the mistletoe kissing, with Hailey's hand held out to the camera, flaunting the giant rock on her finger—a rock that should've been mine!" I looked over at Isla, and she gave me the get-on-with-it eyes. "That night, I had a little too much to drink and decided to make my *own* holiday card. It was a joke. I found a photo of myself from my trip to Aruba and photoshopped in the hot guy I found online. But…" I chewed on my lip. "I wound up finishing the bottle of wine while I printed out the fake holiday card, and then…I walked to the mailbox at two in the morning and mailed it! *I mailed it to Davis, Isla!* The next day I went to the post office and tried to get them to give it back to me, but they wouldn't."

Isla's eyes bulged. "And that guy is here? The guy you photoshopped in?"

I nodded. "I'm pretty sure it's him."

"Which one?"

I lifted my chin toward the man who looked like he'd walked out of an Abercrombie ad. "The guy in the navy sweater."

"Damn. He's pretty."

I covered my forehead, feeling clammy. "What am I going to do?"

"First off, you're going to calm down. Because there is no way in hell some random, gorgeous guy you found on the Internet just walked into this stuffy party. And even if it is him—which I sincerely doubt it is—who's going to know? You only sent the card to Davis, right?"

I nodded.

"It was a year ago. So even if it were him, there's no way Davis would remember now."

Everything Isla said was logical, yet I still wanted to throw up. I shook my head. "I don't know, Isla. It definitely looks like him."

"It's not. Stop freaking out. You probably don't even remember yourself. You were drunk, and it was a full year ago."

Maybe she was right. Maybe I didn't remember. I'd probably seen this guy on social media—he obviously had a connection to Davis if he was here. And maybe that face stuck with me because he *resembled* the guy I'd photoshopped. I mean, what would that random man I found be doing at Davis's Christmas party anyway? I knew almost all of the people who usually came.

My heart rate slowed.

Isla was right. I was being ridiculous.

This man wasn't my fake boyfriend. I'd been drunk that night, and now I was just confused.

Yeah, that's it.

I almost started to believe it. Though I still held my breath as I watched my ex walk over to the two guys who'd just come in. The three of them spoke for a moment, and then Davis scanned the room. When he found me, he pointed.

My eyes widened. "Oh no..."

Davis and my fake boyfriend started to walk in my direction. I wanted to head for the hills, run away from the train wreck about to happen. But I couldn't move. My legs were paralyzed from fear, and my feet felt like concrete blocks.

Davis smiled as he approached. "Hey, Joy. Hey, Isla. Look who I just met? It took me a few seconds to place the face, but then I remembered your Christmas card last year."

Abercrombie Guy's brows drew together. He looked at me, then Davis, then back to me. I had no idea what the hell to do, so I decided to go with it.

I threw my arms around the man and planted a chaste kiss square on his mouth. "Hi, honey. I didn't think you were going to be able to make it."

CHAPTER 2

Nolan

The brown-haired beauty glared at me, a silent prompt to go along with this, whatever the hell was going on. I guess it was showtime.

"My business dinner got canceled," I began slowly. "So...I was able to make it after all."

She breathed a sigh of relief.

The guy held out his hand. "Probably should've introduced myself formally. Davis Lawson. Nice to meet you, Nolan."

He knows my name? I never told him. "How did...you know my name?"

"Well, we have that picture of you here on our fridge, the one with your abs hanging out. I use it for motivation to hit the weights." He smacked my arm.

This night just keeps getting weirder.

I narrowed my eyes. "I'm...on your fridge?"

"The Christmas card from last year," Davis said. "You and Joy in Aruba."

"Ah." My eyes widened as I turned to her. *Joy.* At least I had her name now. I scratched my chin. "Right. How could I forget? Bermuda. Great trip. Good rum."

Joy's face reddened. "*Aruba…*"

I snapped my fingers. "Sorry, yeah."

Davis looked between us. "Joy never actually told me how you two met…"

She smiled at me through gritted teeth as she said nothing. She wanted *me* to pull something out of my ass? *Okay.*

"We were in one of those cat cafés," I blurted. "You know, the ones in Tokyo? Where the cats roam the place and you can pet them?"

Joy's fake smile faded.

Davis turned to her. "I never knew you went to Tokyo?"

Joy pushed a piece of hair behind her ear. "It was a last-minute thing." She cleared her throat. "Got a good deal the summer before last. Remember when I took that random week off? I was in Tokyo, actually."

"I'll never forget the moment I first saw her." I grinned, having a bit more fun with this as each second passed. "Do you remember that, babe?"

"Yeah." She laughed nervously. "There were…so many…cats."

I shook my head. "*So* many fucking cats. And they were all gravitating toward you." I turned to Davis. "I could barely see her because she was buried under them."

Davis's brow furrowed. "That sounds quite terrifying, actually."

"Turned out she was sitting on a pillow filled with cat-nip," I added. "When Joy figured it out, she moved over to the seat next to me. And that's when I became the luckiest man alive."

Joy chuckled. "It was purrr-fect."

I frowned at her. *That was bad.*

She shrugged.

Davis's eyes veered to a corner of the room. "Well, you two have fun. I have to say hello to one of the guys from the office. Catch you in a bit."

"Yeah..." I said, watching him walk away.

"Cats?" Joy nudged me with her elbow. "What the hell?"

"What? You're surprised I made up a ridiculous story? Apparently, *you're* the one with some explaining to do." I looked around. "Actually, where's the kitchen?"

"Why?" She followed me as I weaved through the crowd.

"I need to see this Christmas card he thinks I'm on."

Sure enough, smack dab in the middle of their expensive, stainless-steel fridge was my smiling face. I remembered that day. That photo of me had been taken in Laguna Beach when I visited one of my college buddies. Except now I was standing next to a bikini-clad Joy in Aruba, evidently.

I removed the magnet and held the card up. "You even matched your bikini to my shorts. Are we one of those annoying couples who dress alike?"

Joy let out a long breath and looked down at her shoes. "I'm really sorry, Nolan. This is extremely embarrassing."

Despite the nutty thing she'd done, I instinctually felt she wasn't at all crazy. Maybe just...vulnerable or something. There had to be a damn good reason why she'd gone to such lengths.

I placed the card back on the refrigerator, my tone softening. "Wanna talk about it?"

Joy smiled sadly, and over the next few minutes proceeded to explain how she'd come across my Instagram one day and gotten the bright idea to make the fake card, sending it to her ex. He was apparently dating a coworker of theirs now. I could understand wanting to make him jealous under the circumstances.

"I have to give you credit. You did a damn good job on the photoshop," I said.

"Thanks." She laughed. "I think."

"Anyway…" I held out my hand. "I'd like to officially introduce myself. I'm Nolan Bradstreet."

"Joy Hannigan." She took my hand. "If you don't know Davis, how did you end up here?"

"A friend of mine is a friend of Davis's. Ben dragged me here. Except I have no idea where the hell he is at the moment. I'm really just here for the free booze. Didn't think I'd be meeting my fake girlfriend tonight. That's for damn sure."

She sighed. "Gosh, I guess I lucked out that you'd never met Davis through your friend, then. That would've been a disaster." Joy laughed. "Well, even *more* of a disaster." Her face reddened. "God, I owe you an apology."

"No need." I placed my hand on her arm. "Truly. I get why you did what you did. And I'm sure you never imagined you'd meet me."

"You can bet on that." She exhaled. "I could really use a drink. Care to join me?"

I winked. "Well, it would look a little weird to Davis if I abandoned my girl now, wouldn't it?"

Joy and I walked together over to the bar. After we got our drinks, she pierced a maraschino cherry with a toothpick and popped it into her mouth. "So, what do you do, Nolan?"

I arched a brow. "You don't already know?"

"Okay…" she conceded. "I might've seen a few posts about your job on your page." She shrugged. "How are things going at Seaver Pharmaceuticals?"

"Good…good." I nodded. "It's a lot of traveling, but I like it."

"Go anywhere interesting lately? Besides cat cafés in Tokyo?"

"I actually *did* go to Tokyo for business. Even went to one of the cat cafés. Just never met a beautiful woman there." *Okay, am I seriously flirting now?* This night kept evolving into the unexpected. I sipped my beer. "What do *you* do?"

"I work at Pride Bank with Davis. He's a vice president, and I work in customer relations."

"Sounds…" I hesitated.

"Pretty boring, actually." She laughed.

Not gonna argue that. "So, that must be weird working with your ex *and* his new girlfriend, huh?" I looked around. "Is she here?"

Joy pointed her chin toward the left corner of the room. "She's the one over there with the hyena laugh."

I turned to check out the brunette in the corner who had nothing on the beautiful woman in front of me. "I'm guessing there are still feelings there on your part, if you went through all the trouble of making a fake holiday card?"

Joy shook her head. "It wasn't about that. It was more about…appearances."

Hmm… I wasn't sure if I bought that.

A text chimed on my phone, reminding me of the time. *Shit.*

"What's wrong?"

"I'm so sorry, Joy. I have to leave. I'm late."

"Late for what?"

Oh, the irony. I hated leaving her when we were just getting to know each other. But considering where I was headed, it would've been an asshole move to ask for her number.

"I have a date."

CHAPTER 3

Joy

I very rarely went on Facebook anymore. But the following Saturday night I was home and bored, so I clicked to see who had gotten engaged or pregnant this month. I wasn't even bitter about it—but seriously, every time I turned around, someone was flashing a ring, wearing a white dress, or holding up a sonogram picture. I guess this was what al-most-thirty looked like. At least to everyone else.

I took a deep breath as I signed on, preparing to be hit with someone's *happy news* while I sat at home drinking a glass of wine by myself. But to my surprise, what popped up made my heart race in a good way.

Nolan Bradstreet wants to confirm your relation-ship.

Our relationship, though? I was excited to see that my gorgeous, fake boyfriend had made contact, but I had no idea what relationship he could possibly be confirming until I clicked into the notification.

Nolan Bradstreet listed you as in a relationship. Please confirm to update your new status.

I cracked up. How fortunate that my fake boyfriend has a good sense of humor. Most guys would never have gone along with my madness at Davis's party. They would've bolted as quickly as possible. I was more than happy to confirm my new status, so I clicked accept. After, a box popped up telling me Nolan and I were also now Facebook friends. That news was just as exciting, because I had access to his private photos. My bleak Saturday night suddenly became a bit brighter, and I couldn't start perusing fast enough.

I took another gulp of my wine as I opened up the first album, and I almost spit sauvignon blanc all over my laptop when I got a look at the first picture. "Holy crap," I said out loud. "He's as off his rocker as I am!" Nolan hadn't just made us Facebook official with a status update, he'd posted a picture of us! And in a cat café in Tokyo, no less. He'd tagged Café Termari no Ouchi in the photo, too.

Oh my God. I couldn't stop smiling as I stared at the screen. This man was certifiable, and I freaking *loved* it! The best part was that he clearly had *no* photoshop skills. I recognized the photo of me as one I'd posted last year on Isla's twenty-ninth birthday. We'd been standing arm in arm, but he'd cut her out so it was just me, only he'd failed to remove three of Isla's fingers from the front of my waist. The caption read: *I love you meow and furever, Joy Hannigan.*

I stared at the photo, with my hand covering an enormous smile, for a full five minutes. Not only was the man funny and playful, he was even more gorgeous than I remembered. Dark hair, smooth tan skin, and light green eyes that almost didn't look real. Not to mention, his jawline rivaled Matt Bomer's. I was jealous of the cat in his hands.

Eventually, I clicked on the rest of his photos, figuring I'd check out his friends and family, see what he does for fun, and maybe find out what type of women he tended to go for. But the second picture I clicked on was *also* of us. In fact, there were four more of them! I laughed my way through each and every one.

Us at the Bronx Zoo, standing in front of the lion's cage. We were obviously both photoshopped into that one. I'm guessing Nolan took his photo from some sort of sporting event, since he was holding a giant Styrofoam finger. With a super-quick glance, he might've gotten away with people believing the photo was real, except I was *barefoot* in my picture! Who goes to the Bronx Zoo without shoes?

Us dressed in costumes. Oh my God. Did he dress up as Wayne from *Wayne's World* to match that photo of me dressed as Garth from two years ago? Or had he really been Wayne for Halloween at some point?

Us at the beach. That one looked pretty good. Except... I leaned in for a closer look. Did he make my boobs bigger? I was pretty certain he'd turned my C cups into double Ds.

The last one was an actual photo—the one he'd snapped for posterity before he left Davis's Christmas party. I'd been kicking myself in the ass over the last week for not taking one, too.

Those photos were so much fun that I was a little disappointed when I stalked his regular ones. After I got to the end of his last album, I decided to message my Facebook-official fake boyfriend.

Joy: Hey. Just wanted to say that you totally made my day with those photos! I laughed through every single one. But…did I get breast augmentation surgery and forget about it??

It was nine PM on a Saturday night. I figured there was no way in hell he'd be online. But two minutes later, my laptop pinged with an incoming message. My pulse picked up as I opened it.

Nolan: Sorry. I might've done that at three in the morning after too much to drink.

I smiled as I typed back.

Joy: That's exactly how I got myself into this mess last year. Drinking and Facebook. There should be breathalyzers on laptops for when you try to sign on past ten PM.

Nolan: For the record, I was just amusing myself. You look perfect the way you are.

I felt warmth in my cheeks, and it had nothing to do with the wine I lifted to sip.

Joy: I actually Googled cat cafés in Tokyo this week. I can't believe how many there are. And there are some bars, too!

Nolan: Yeah, it was an experience. Apparently they started because most apartments in Japan don't allow pets. Did you know we have a few here in the city?

Joy: Really?

Nolan: I've never been. But when I posted a photo from my trip, a few people told me they'd been to Meow Parlour. It's on the Lower East Side somewhere.

For the next hour and a half, Nolan and I chatted on Messenger. Our conversation flowed easily, and a few times I thought he was even flirting with me. Though I couldn't be sure, because the guy clearly had a playful personality. I poured a second glass of wine and finished it off while we got to know each other, but this time I limited myself to two so I didn't say or do something else stupid.

Nolan: So what do you do for Christmas? I can't believe it's in five days. Wasn't it just Halloween last week? Nice Garth, by the way.

Joy: My friend Isla, who you met at the party, was Wayne. Did you actually dress as Wayne, too, or did you just do that for the photo? I go to my sister's for Christmas. She has two kids, so it's always fun—unlike my parents' annual holiday party on Christmas Eve. That I dread.

Nolan: Nope. I was Wayne last year when I was forced to go to a party where everyone had to dress as famous couples. Why the dread for your parents' party?

Joy: Great minds think alike. And I love my parents. They're amazing people, but my mom thinks I'm going to die an old maid since Davis and I broke up. Anytime she has people over, she now happens to invite a single guy. I'm not looking forward to meeting this year's hot commodity. Last year, the guy I was stuck talking to half the

night was obsessed with Deadliest Catch. He spent an hour telling me about each episode of the new season. And I'm allergic to shellfish!

Nolan: Oh, man. Why don't you bring the holiday card to show them you have a new boyfriend? Or better yet, mail them one!

I laughed out loud.

Joy: I couldn't do that. I'm really close to my mom. She would know if I had a boyfriend serious enough to put on a holiday card. That trick only worked on Davis.

However, maybe if I *brought* my own boyfriend to the party, they wouldn't think they constantly needed to fix me up. Would it be insane to ask Nolan to go with me? I chewed my lip, debating. He'd said he had a *date* the night of Davis's party—not a girlfriend. And Nolan seemed like a fun guy who was up for anything. I bet we'd have a blast being a fake couple again. Plus...maybe there would be an opportunity for a second kiss. Lord knows I hadn't stopped thinking about the first one. So I said *screw it* and started typing before I changed my mind.

Joy: Any chance you're free on Christmas Eve? Maybe you can come to my parents' party and play the role of fake boyfriend again—help them get off my back about dating.

A long pause went by, way longer than the time between our messages had been, so I started to grow anxious. Then the text came in.

Nolan: I wish I could. But I already have plans. I told Kylie, the girl I went out with the night of Davis's party, that I'd go to see A Christmas Carol with her.

Two days later, I woke to another tag on Facebook. Nolan had honed his photoshop skills and made some more photos of us. They were definitely better, but still pretty funny. Though the novelty had lost its luster since I was rejected, and the last couple days I'd been walking around with a hollow feeling in the pit of my stomach.

Later in the afternoon, I opened my laptop to do some last-minute online Christmas shopping from the office, and I found a new message from Nolan.

Nolan: How did I do with the new photos? I think I'm almost ready to make my own card.

I smiled, but that hollow feeling hit me again. I'd essentially kissed this man, then asked him out, and he'd rejected me. Worse, I really liked him. There was no use torturing myself when he wasn't into me, so I didn't bother to respond. Instead, I shut my laptop and decided to brave the stores in person on my way home from work.

A little while later, I walked out of the building, still feeling glum, only to run straight into Davis and his fiancée. They were all smiles and kissy faces. I attempted to slink away without them seeing me, but failed.

"Joy!" Davis yelled.

I turned and forced a smile. "Oh, hi. I didn't see you guys."

"I'm glad we ran into you. I've been meaning to come talk to you."

"Oh?"

"Hailey and I are going out to dinner this weekend, on the twenty-seventh, with Ben and his girlfriend."

"Ben?"

"The guy Nolan came to the party with."

I nodded. "Oh, right."

"Why don't you and Nolan join us?"

My face fell. Davis noticed and held up his hands.

"Unless that's too weird? Maybe it is…"

I had no choice but to force a smile back on my face, though I didn't have the energy to come up with an excuse as to why Nolan and I couldn't make it. So I took the easy route and figured I'd cancel via text in a day or two.

"Sure. That sounds great."

Davis smiled. "Oh good. I'm glad you don't think it's weird."

How could I? Dinner with my ex and his fiancée wasn't half as weird as photoshopping a stranger into your Christmas card and pretending he's your boyfriend.

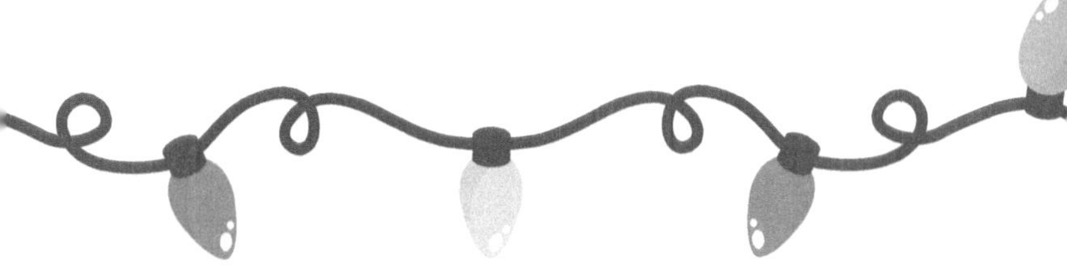

CHAPTER 4

Nolan

I was out to lunch with my buddy Tim on Christmas Eve when I noticed a familiar face coming into the restaurant.

"Crap," I muttered.

"What?" Tim asked.

"Nothing." I shook my head. "There's just...someone I know over there."

Before I could say anything else, Joy's ex, Davis, spotted me and came over to our table.

Straightening in my seat, I feigned a smile. "Hey, man. Good to see you again..." *God, I want to punch that guy.*

"You too." He looked between Tim and me. "Hailey and I were supposed to go out with you and Joy this weekend, but she texted me to cancel already. I'm sorry you can't make it."

Hmm... "Oh yeah? What did she say?"

"Just that you two had a lot of holiday plans already and maybe we could do a raincheck after the new year. I was bummed because your buddy Ben and his girlfriend are coming, too. Figured the six of us would have a good time."

Thankfully, I'd confided in Ben about Joy's lie. Otherwise, he would've been hella confused. Scratching my chin, I said, "I see."

I wondered why Joy had never asked me to accompany her. I totally would've gone.

"Anyway," he said, "talk to her and see what works for you guys after the new year. Would still love to get together."

I nodded. "Will do."

After Davis walked out of earshot, Tim narrowed his eyes, looking understandably confused. "Um...am I missing something here? Since when do you have a girlfriend named Joy?"

I chuckled. "Clearly you haven't been on social media lately."

He took out his phone. "Let me look at your page..."

Tim's eyes widened after he pulled up my profile. He began scrolling through all the fake photos I'd generated. "Okay. Wow. She's a smokeshow. Why didn't you say anything?"

"Well, for one, because none of it's real."

"She's AI?" He laughed.

"No."

He squinted. "What the hell are you talking about, then?"

"Joy is a real person. And that's really her. But every single one of those photos is photoshopped. We were never together. Not bad, right?"

His eyes widened, and I spent the next several minutes explaining the Joy situation from the beginning.

"That's some wacky shit." He paused. "Okay, wait. When we met up here today, you mentioned you had a date tonight that you weren't all that excited about. Are you telling me that's with someone else and not the woman in these photos?"

I chomped on some ice. "Correct."

"So, if you're not pumped about that date, why the hell aren't you going out with Joy instead for real? You said she's single, right?"

I sighed. "I don't get the impression she's ready for anything right now."

He arched a brow. "Based on what?"

"Well, for one, she's clearly not over that guy Davis. She's still keeping up this façade. If she didn't give a shit, wouldn't she just tell him the truth? Or at least break up with me?"

Break up with me? I sounded like a lunatic.

"So she's trying to make him jealous. What's *your* excuse for feeding into this charade?"

"I told you, I'm just doing it to entertain her at this point."

Tim smirked. "Because you *like* her…"

"Well, yeah. But I don't expect anything to come of it."

I did like her—a lot. If I were being honest, there was more to my hesitancy than I was letting on. *I* was afraid to get involved with someone who was still hung up on someone else. Engaged or not, it was only a matter of time before that idiot Davis came to his senses and begged her to take him back. The woman really seemed like the full package. And if she jumped on that, where would it leave me?

He chuckled. "Well, too bad it's not real. She's freakin' smokin', man." He tilted his head. "If you're not technically dating her, you mind setting your boy here up? I mean, I have no qualms about her still being hung up on that dork we just met. I'd snap her out of that real fast."

My face felt hot. "Yeah. Not gonna happen."

Damn. What was up with my reaction? Tim's suggestion had made me feel flat-out jealous. I did really like Joy.

Later that night, I'd finished getting ready for my date with Kylie and had some time to kill before I had to meet her downtown.

I'd made sure to block Kylie from my posts on social media so she wouldn't get the wrong idea about Joy and me—not that Kylie and I were even seriously dating. This would only be our second get together, the first of which was the night I'd met Joy. I remembered being totally distracted, thinking about the woman I'd met at Davis's party rather than the one right in front of me that night.

I decided to log on and check my page to see if Joy had posted anything new or liked any of my posts. She'd done neither. Was she over the whole thing or just busy? Since she hadn't said anything about the last few doctored photos, I decided maybe they weren't good enough. I needed to up my game.

I found a photo of a couple sitting in a horse-drawn carriage in the middle of Times Square. After inserting Joy's and my heads onto the respective people, I made up an elaborate story to go along with the post. It was all about how our horse had gotten spooked by a loud noise, veering off its path to end up in the middle of all the hustle and bustle of Times Square. In the next photo, we were ice skating at Rockefeller Center, followed by an image of us standing in front of Radio City Music Hall. Boy, we'd been busy—and really getting into the holiday spirit.

I sent her a quick message.

Nolan: Check out what we've been up to lately. ;-)

I exited out before calling a ride to head downtown.

Just as the car was about to drop me off at my destination, I checked to see if Joy had written.

My message had been seen a half hour ago—but no response.

CHAPTER 5

Nolan

It was really bugging me that Joy had read my messages and didn't respond.

As soon as *A Christmas Carol* was over, I dug my phone out of my pocket. My date noticed.

"Is everything okay? You checked your messages a half dozen times before the show started."

Shit. I hadn't meant to be rude about it, especially since Kylie had treated me to the play we'd just watched. She'd refused to let me give her any money for the tickets. I shoved my phone back into my pocket, intent on giving her the attention she deserved.

"Sorry. Bad habit. Just a work thing going on."

"No problem. I'm guilty of it, too. Especially when a patient I get friendly with isn't doing well."

"A patient?"

Her brows furrowed. "I'm a nurse. Remember?"

I actually hadn't. I'd been on two dates with this very nice woman, and my head had been somewhere else both times. It seemed to be a running problem of mine lately—

all Joy, all the time. I didn't even want to guess how many hours I'd spent photoshopping, and when I wasn't looking at pictures of Joy, somehow thoughts of her kept crossing my mind.

"Of course. Sorry."

Kylie shrugged it off. "Would you want to go over to Serendipity? I love their frozen hot chocolate."

The last place I wanted to be during the holidays was Times Square. It was a touristy nightmare. But I owed her for all the times I'd been mentally checked out. So I put my hand on her back. "That sounds great. Let's go."

An hour later, Kylie seemed happy that she'd gotten her frozen hot chocolate. I wasn't really hungry, but I'd ordered a piece of humble pie since I could never turn down anything made with peanut butter.

Kylie was telling me how she was thinking of going back to school to become a nurse practitioner when my phone buzzed on the table. I looked at it, but stopped myself from reaching out to pick it up while she was talking. A few minutes later though, it buzzed a second time. I was *itching* to know if the notification was Joy messaging me back, but again, I somehow managed to resist. The third time it happened, Kylie put me out of my misery.

"Will you excuse me?" she said. "I need to go to the ladies' room."

I stood as she got up from her chair. "Of course."

The minute she turned her back and started toward the restroom, I reached for my phone. Disappointment set in when I saw the message was from a friend at work and not Joy. I even opened up the Facebook app and checked to see if she'd messaged me and I'd missed the notification. But only the *read* notification on my message to her greeted me—a reminder that Joy had seen my message four hours ago and still not responded.

The woman who was *actually* interested in me returned from the ladies' room a few minutes later. I stood as she took her seat, but when I went to sit back down, a table on the other side of the room caught my eye. *That couldn't be.* Could it?

But it really looked like Isla—Joy's friend she'd been with at the party the weekend before last. Was I imagining things now? I had to be. More than eight-million people lived in New York City. What were the chances I'd run into Joy's ex and her friend on the same day? Though the longer I stared, the more I felt certain it was her. This wasn't good, considering I'd already been having trouble concentrating on my date. There was no way in hell I'd be able to pay attention now without finding out if that was actually Isla. Especially not once she got up from her table and started to walk toward the hall that led to the ladies' room.

So I told a white lie. "Sorry. It's my turn now. I need to hit the head."

"Oh. Sure."

I had no idea what I was going to say or do if it was Isla, yet my legs started moving rapidly nonetheless. By the time I made it to the hallway where the bathrooms were, she was already in the ladies' room. I had no choice but to hang around like a stalker waiting for his prey. When the woman walked out of the restroom, I feigned my best surprised face.

"Hey. Isla, right? Joy's friend?"

She smiled. "Yep. Hey, Nolan. I thought that might be you, but I didn't want to interrupt your date." She paused. "Though...it sort of looked like you might've been happy if I had."

"What's that supposed to mean?"

She shrugged. "You just looked bored, that's all."

I sighed. "I thought I was better at hiding it. My mind is elsewhere tonight."

"It happens. The holidays are such a busy time."

"Actually, it's not Christmas that has me distracted. It's your friend Joy."

"Really? Then why the heck didn't you say yes when she asked you out?"

"She didn't ask me out."

"She said she asked you to go to her parents' Christmas party, and you said no."

My brows furrowed. "I had plans, and I didn't think that was a date. I thought she was just asking me to play a role, pretend to be her boyfriend for the sake of her parents."

Isla rolled her eyes. "*Duh*. That's because it's not easy for a woman to ask out a man. She hasn't shut up about you since her dumbass ex's Christmas party."

I smiled. "He is a dope, isn't he?"

Isla put her hands on her hips. "It seems he's not the only one. I don't get it. If you can't stop thinking about her, why didn't you ask her out for another night?"

"I didn't think she was over her ex. She made that card and went to his Christmas party and everything."

"My best friend is pretty much perfect, except for one big flaw. She gives a shit what people think *waay* too much. Joy goes to that boring party every year because she and Davis and his new fiancée all work together, and she thinks if she *doesn't* go, people at work will start gossiping that she's still hung up on him." Isla shook her head. "It's so dumb, I know."

"She's really over him, though?"

"She has been for a very long time."

Fuck. I'm a total idiot.

Isla smiled. "Well, it looks like you got one thing right, at least."

"What's that?"

"I can see on your face that you're kicking yourself in the ass right now for making such a stupid decision." She put a hand on my shoulder. "You want my advice?"

"Yes."

"Grow a pair." Isla smiled. "I need to get back to my cousin. Have a merry Christmas, Nolan."

I returned to my date, but it was even more impossible to concentrate now. The waitress came with the bill, and I was relieved to be able to call it a night. I left cash in the padfolio and walked to the door with Kylie. But once we were outside on the street, I couldn't make myself move. So I told *another* white lie to my very nice date. "I'm sorry. I forgot something on the table. I'll be right back."

Inside, I made a beeline back to Isla's table.

She smiled as I approached and leaned back in her chair. "Grow them this fast?"

"Do you know what time Joy's parents' party usually goes to?"

"Probably about eleven."

I took a deep breath and looked at my watch. "Can I have the address?"

"You're not going to bring your date, are you?"

"No. I'm going to do the right thing and be honest with her."

Isla's smile widened. "One twenty-five Liberty Street. Hoboken."

Back outside, Kylie hooked her arm with mine. She seemed oblivious, even though Isla had been able to see I was bored from across the restaurant. I guess sometimes it's easier to see the forest than the trees. I lifted my arm to stop a passing taxi.

Kylie tilted her head as I opened the cab door. "Do you want to go back to your place?"

"I had a really nice time, and I think you're a great person, but I have to be honest and tell you I don't think it's going to work out."

Her face fell. "Oh."

"I'm sorry."

"Well, I'm disappointed, but I'd rather know how you feel now than after getting in deeper."

"I really am sorry."

She shrugged. "No biggie. I guess this is goodbye then?"

I nodded. "You take the cab."

"Actually…" She pointed up the block. "I have a friend who works at the bar on the corner. I'm going to stop in there for a drink. Take care of yourself, Nolan."

"You, too, Kylie."

The cabbie was still waiting, so I jumped in.

"Where to?"

"One twenty-five Liberty Street. Hoboken. And if you step on it and get me there before eleven, I'll pay you double."

CHAPTER 6

Joy

"Well, I certainly can't blame you for picking him." My grandmother handed me back my phone.

We were in our own corner of the living room at my parents' holiday party. I'd just finished showing Grandma some of the doctored photos Nolan had been posting after telling her the story of my holiday-card fiasco. Grandma and I had a very honest relationship, and she was the only person here I felt comfortable admitting everything to.

"Why did you stop responding to him?" she asked. "Seems like he's been trying hard to get your attention."

I sighed. "I feel like he's just having fun and is not really interested in more with me. Plus, he's dating someone else. So why bother entertaining anything when I'll only end up disappointed?" I shook my head. "I regret even starting this whole thing."

My grandmother sipped her spiked eggnog. "You know, before I lost your granddad, I always thought I'd need a man to be happy. And while I miss him like crazy, I wouldn't dream of dealing with anyone else now. I'm happy being by myself, enjoying my life without having to answer to anyone. I know you're in a much different place than an eighty-year-old woman, but one day, maybe after you have kids and a family of your own, you might look back at this time in your life and miss the independence. So make the most of it. Be proud of it." She lifted her cup in a salute. "Screw these guys." She chuckled. "Okay, maybe only Davis. Fuck Davis. The other one seems to be funny and a sweetheart."

I cackled. When my grandmother said the F-word, you knew it was serious. Grandma had never liked my ex, never believed he was good enough for me. He was, in her words, "a tool." Her feelings had only escalated when she'd found out he was dating someone from the office. Her advice tonight, though, had shed light on the reality of the situation. Being attached to someone else isn't what gives a person value. And you don't need to rely on another person to find happiness.

"You're so right. I'm a successful woman. I'm healthy. I don't have to lie about my life to make it seem better—not to Davis or to anyone else. As long as *I'm* happy, it doesn't matter what anyone else thinks."

"Learning not to give a fuck comes with age, baby. It's okay if you make mistakes along the way. You're still young."

"Thanks for the kick in the ass, Grandma." I lifted my eggnog. "Fuck Davis!"

My grandmother and I were both laughing when my phone chimed a moment later.

Davis: Merry Christmas. Hope you're having a good night. Tell Nolan I said hello.

I cracked up again. He must've sensed us talking about him.

I couldn't type fast enough.

Joy: Merry Christmas! Nolan and I broke up.

The three dots moved around as he responded.

Davis: Gosh. Really? At Christmas time, too. I'm so sorry to hear that.

Joy: Don't be sorry. I'm happier than I've ever been. That's been the case ever since our breakup, to be honest. Don't take it personally. I'm happy you're happy now too. Everything has happened the way it was meant to.

Davis: Well, I'm glad for you then.

Joy: You have a good Christmas Eve with Hailey.

Davis: Thank you. You have a good one as well.

It felt so freeing to have "broken up" with Nolan, thus ridding myself of the lie I'd created.

There was only one problem. While I now realized I no longer needed a boyfriend for appearances, I did miss talking to Nolan for no other reason than he made me smile. And he certainly wasn't bad to look at, either. I wished he and I had met under different circumstances. It would've also been nice if he weren't dating someone.

But it was Christmas Eve, and I didn't want to spend the rest of this night looking back at all of the things I regretted in the past year. I vowed to do better in the new year and truly embrace the freedom I had now to do whatever I wanted. Go wherever I wanted. Maybe a cat café in Tokyo—but for real this time. The world was my oyster!

Later, I was preparing a plate of food for myself at the buffet table when I heard a commotion over by the front door.

The next thing I knew, my grandmother came traipsing toward me in her ugly Christmas sweater holding a handsome man's hand. Not any man. *My* man. Well, my *fake* man.

Oh my God.

I nearly dropped my food.

"Stolen Nolan is just as handsome in person!" Grandma announced.

I felt my face heat as I set my plate down. *What is he doing here?*

"What...how?" I asked as Nolan stood in front of me, smelling like heaven mixed with the cold air outside. It felt like there was a spotlight on us as my entire family gawked.

"I ran into Isla. She gave me your address." Nolan smiled. "Can we go somewhere and talk?"

"Sure. Follow me."

I led him to a room at the back of the house where my mother mostly stored her sewing supplies.

After I closed the door behind us, he said, "Why did you stop responding to my messages?"

"I didn't think you cared all that much." I tilted my head. "Aren't you dating someone?"

"I went on a couple of dates with a woman, but that's over."

My heartbeat sped up a little. "Oh."

"The truth is, I haven't been able to stop thinking about you, Joy. I've just been apprehensive to bite the bullet because I thought you were still hung up on Davis. But after talking to Isla tonight, I no longer believe that."

Not sure what the hell my friend said, but I needed to thank her big time.

"The only man I've been hung up on lately is the real one behind my fake boyfriend," I admitted.

He inched closer. "You know, I've imagined us doing *a lot* of things together, but there's one thing I'd like more than anything."

"What?"

Nolan placed his hands around my face, bringing me in for a kiss. It was everything I remembered—firm and powerful. As he slipped his tongue into my mouth, I began to dig my fingers into his beautiful mane of dark hair. My nerve endings lit up like a Christmas tree. The sounds coming from the party faded into the distance as we continued to kiss passionately, getting lost in each other.

When Nolan and I finally emerged from the back room, his hair was tousled. I took a few moments to brush through it with my fingers before we reappeared in the living room.

I had no choice but to formally introduce him to my curious family.

Clearing my throat, I said, "Everyone, this is Nolan, my…" I hesitated. *What is he exactly?*

Nolan finished my sentence. "Joy and I just started dating a few minutes ago, but I swear it feels more like a year."

I shrugged. Seemed an accurate description to me.

Nolan spent the next several minutes meeting my parents and relatives. And Grandma gave him the official seal of approval. It was a strange first date, but our entire history had been strange thus far. We'd been through a lot virtually together, but *this* was truly the beginning.

After the introductions were over, we stole a private moment by the Christmas tree.

Nolan took out his camera and snapped a selfie of us.

He winked. "For next year's Christmas card."

THE END

The Twelve Dates of Christmas

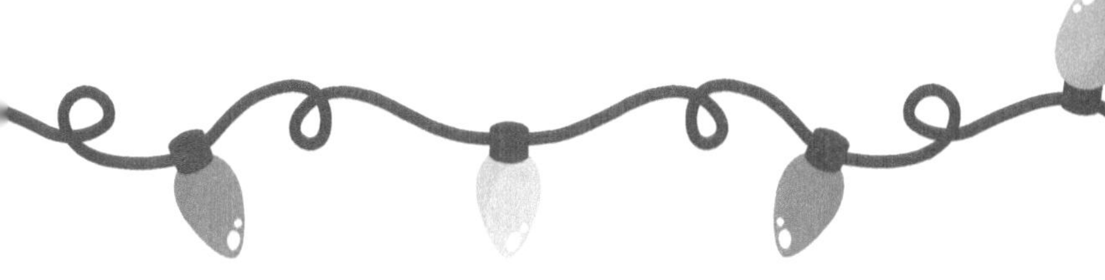

CHAPTER 1

Tucker

"What the heck is going on in here?" Lucy plopped her purse on top of the bar and slid onto a stool. "Was there a funeral across the street at Morrow and the attendees all came over here after or something?"

I chuckled and wiped down the counter in front of her. "No such luck. This is your buddy's doing."

"These people are here for Maggie?"

"Yep."

"Why?"

I reached behind the counter and grabbed the flyer my sister had sprung on me an hour before the crowd started to pile in tonight.

Lucy scanned it. "The Twelve Dates of Christmas? She's doing one of her dating events here at The Rusty Nail?"

I shrugged. "Apparently so."

"And you're okay with that?"

I stopped wiping the counter and caught Lucy's eyes. "What do you think?"

Her lip twitched. "Got it." Lucy swiveled around to check out the suits that had taken over my little local bar.

Sleepy Hollow was a small town thirty miles outside of New York City, so luckily, we didn't get these types in here too often. My regulars were mostly construction workers and firefighters—and I didn't mind that one bit. I also didn't mind our usual lack of decorations. But today, my sister had transformed the bar into a holiday explosion, covering every inch in lights, fake snow, and garland. The glittery tinsel dangling from the ceiling gave me a headache.

I lifted my chin when Lucy turned back. "You want your usual?"

"Yes, please." She smiled, and my eyes lingered on her mouth for an extra heartbeat, the same way they had for the last decade. Lucy Snow had been my sister's best friend since elementary school. I'd known her practically my whole life, but I'd first *noticed her* when I was eleven and she was fifteen. I'll never forget the red, white, and blue bikini she wore the summer I was going into sixth grade. The top was red with white stars and the bottom was blue with stripes. I'd saluted her patriotism every time I peered out my bedroom window at the pool in our yard, though not with my hand.

I poured Lucy her usual, a glass of Amici sauvignon blanc, and returned to find my sister's ass parked on the stool next to her friend.

"Isn't this great?" Maggie beamed. "Look at all the business we're getting."

I frowned. "It'll probably scare the locals away."

"*Or* it might make them think there's a *reason* to come in here. This place is usually dead on a Thursday night at six o'clock."

"This place does just fine."

Maggie rolled her eyes. "Whatever. Can you make me an espresso martini, please?"

I squinted. "A what?"

"You're a bartender. Clearly you've heard of an espresso martini before?"

"Of course I have. We just don't make 'em here."

"Who says?"

"I just did. You got shit in your ears?"

"I've decided to have a signature drink for each night of the Twelve Dates of Christmas. Tomorrow is going to be espresso martini night, and I want to make sure your mixology skills are up to par."

"You want espresso martinis, you make 'em. You own half this place, too."

"I need to host the events!"

I shrugged. "Sounds like a *you* problem."

One of the annoying suits walked up to the bar and lifted his chin to me. "Can I have a cucumber martini, please?"

"Sorry, my martini shaker broke. How about a beer?"

He laughed, but when I didn't, he studied my face. "Really?"

"Yep. Was shaking an *espresso martini* last week, and the bottom just fell out of the shaker. A real tragedy."

The guy's brows pulled together. He still wasn't sure if I was fucking with him or not.

My sister rolled her eyes and stood. "*I'll* make you one, sir. I actually just got a new shaker a little while ago. I had it imported from *Italy*."

The bar got busier after that, mostly because all the New York City people my sister had invited out to Sleepy Hollow for her stupid dating event wanted fancy cocktails that took a long time to make. People who order drinks with more than two ingredients piss me off in general, but the ones who do it on Thursday night—the one night a week I look forward to working because Lucy stops by for wine on her way home—those people piss me off *a lot*.

It was a solid hour before I got to spend any real time at the end of the bar with my favorite patron. I dried my hands on a towel and slung it over my shoulder. "How's work going? You just moved into a new space, right?" I knew she had—I remembered everything Lucy Snow ever told me.

She nodded. "Yeah, over on Main Street. It's quieter. The place I was renting became too loud once that gym moved in next door. They teach six Peloton classes a day with blasting music. It was distracting for my patients."

Unfortunately, our conversation was again interrupted, this time by my sister. She acted like Lucy had come to see *her* or something.

Maggie scooped peanuts from the little bowl on the bar and tossed one in the air, trying to catch it with her mouth open. She missed and didn't bother to pick it up from the floor. "Did you know Lucy got a new patient, Tuck?"

I wasn't sure where this was going. "Oh yeah?"

She smirked. "She lures them in by dating them first."

"Maggie!" Lucy frowned. "I told you that in confidence. And I'm not dating my patients." She looked over at me. "I swear I'm not."

A guy down at the other end of the bar raised his hand, trying to get my attention, but I ignored him and stuck around to hear more about whatever this was. I shrugged. "No worries. Your secret is safe with me. But isn't it against some rule for a therapist to date her patients?"

Maggie's phone vibrated on the bar. She picked it up and hopped down from the stool. "I have to take this call. Be back!"

Lucy was still shaking her head when Maggie disappeared. "I'm not dating my patient. I went out on one date with a guy, and we got to talking—he had a lot of emotional issues he was working through after the death of his mother and a recent breakup. We didn't connect on a romantic level, but we sort of connected on a therapist-patient level, and I gave him some advice on managing his anxiety attacks. The following day he called to ask if it would be okay if he saw me as his therapist."

I grinned. "That's an interesting way to drum up business, Luce. Do you look for the unstable ones on Tinder or is Bumble better for that?"

She picked a peanut from the bowl and chucked it at me. "Shut up."

Maggie came back a minute later. "Anyway, what were we talking about?"

My smile spread to a full-fledged grin. "Lucy dating her patients."

"I am *not* dating my patients!"

"No, she's not," Maggie said. "She's counseling them." My sister pulled her friend in for a hug, still laughing. "I'm joking, of course. But your dating life does kinda suck, honey. Wouldn't you agree?"

Lucy sighed. "What dating life?"

"Exactly. Which is why I signed you up for the Twelve Dates of Christmas."

Lucy and I responded in tandem. "You what?"

"Oh look, there's Peter now." Maggie waved, and a guy wearing a shirt and tie with a vest that *I hated* smiled and walked over.

"Lucy Snow, this is Peter Willet. He's your first date for the Twelve Dates of Christmas." Maggie wiggled her fingers. "You two have fun!"

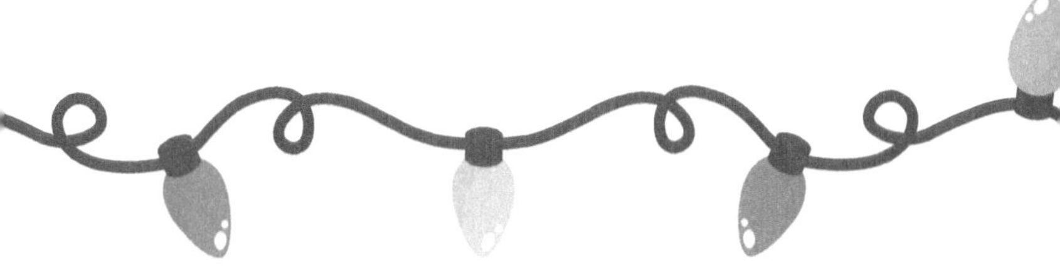

CHAPTER 2

Lucy

I couldn't believe Maggie had roped me into this. Peter might have been handsome, but all he'd done during our date was talk about his boring accounting job.

He took a sip of his drink and gestured toward me. "So, seriously, if you ever need any tricks for deductions, I'm your man."

Maybe he and I could barter services. Peter could be my accountant while I counseled him on how to actually get a life. Maggie had dropped the ball with this one.

We were pretty close to the bar, which meant I was sure Tucker could overhear much of my "date" with Peter. I'd noticed Maggie's hot younger brother glancing over in my direction from time to time. Pretty sad that I'd been locked in on that throughout this date.

At one point Tucker held up a piece of paper with something written in black Sharpie.

Tell him the only thing you want deducted is this dumb date.

Thankfully, Peter's back was facing Tucker. I did everything I could to stifle my laughter as I choked on my drink.

"Is something wrong?" Peter asked.

"No." I coughed. "Sorry. Went down the wrong chute. All is well."

"Ah. Okay." He smiled. "As I was saying, the latest update for Excel has these new features that…" His words faded into the distance as my attention traveled to Tucker once again.

He held up another sheet.

Tell him the only thing he Excels at is boring the snot out of you.

I giggled under my breath and forced my attention toward Peter, despite not processing a word he said.

A few minutes later, Tucker held up a napkin.

Wink if you need help and want out.

I tried to tough it out a little longer, but eventually I decided life was too short to endure dates like this.

The next time I caught Tucker's eye, I winked at him.

It took all of thirty seconds for him to make his way over.

"Excuse me, you wouldn't happen to be Lucy Snow, would you?"

"I am." I faked a look of surprise. "Why?"

"Someone is trying to reach you. Is your cell phone dead or something?"

"Oh goodness." I reached into my purse and pretended to check the battery life. "Yes. I think it is." I stood. "Will you excuse me one moment, Peter?"

"Certainly."

I walked over to the bar and pretended to use Tucker's phone to take the fake call.

After enough time had passed, I walked back over to Peter at our table. "I'm so sorry." I frowned. "I have a bit of a family issue I need to attend to. I'm going to have to cut this date short."

He stood, a look of disappointment on his face. "I'm sorry to hear that. Hope everything is okay?"

"It will be." *After I'm able to get away from you.*

"Well, I certainly hope we can see each other again."

"Thank you for tonight," I said, without committing to anything else. Then I disappeared to a small room located behind the bar.

A minute later, Tucker peeked in. "You good?"

"Yes." I sighed. "Thank you for that."

"I'm keeping an eye out for when he leaves. You can come back when the coast is clear."

As I nodded, I took a moment to appreciate how beautiful Maggie's brother was. Dressed in a fitted black T-shirt that showcased his muscular arms and dark jeans that accentuated his ass, I had to admire the handsome man he'd grown into. He had a few tats on his forearms that only added to his appeal, and his once-short brown hair had grown out a bit. He had just the right amount of chin scruff, which I imagined felt really good against a woman's skin.

"Cool." I cleared my throat. "Thank you, Tucker."

Ten minutes later, he came back to let me know it was safe to return.

When I found a seat at the bar, waiting for me was one of my favorite drinks. "How did you know I wanted a tequila and soda with lime?"

He winked. "That was always your favorite, wasn't it?"

I nodded. "It was pretty much all I drank back in the day—when your sister had parties while your parents were away."

"I remember." He grinned and winked again. "It's on the house, of course."

"Thank you."

"I think you deserve it after enduring that date."

I exhaled. "Thanks again for rescuing me."

"I wouldn't have had to if Maggie hadn't had the brilliant idea to invade the bar with boring suits tonight."

"Well, we both have a right to be annoyed with her, then."

"Let's give her hell when she comes back." He snickered.

His teeth gleamed. I remembered when he wore braces. It felt kind of wrong to be having these feelings about him. But it was hard not to notice. And while the four-year age difference between us had seemed pretty big when we were younger, when you're twenty-nine and twenty-five, not so much.

I stirred the small straw around in my drink. "Maggie means well, though."

He wiped down the bar. "Can I ask you a personal question?"

"This isn't about underwear, is it?" I winked.

Once, when Tucker was ten and his friends were playing Truth or Dare, they'd dared him to ask me what color underwear I was wearing. At the time, I was fourteen and mortified. Pretty sure if he asked me that question now, I'd be okay with it. Especially in that sexy voice. *What are you wearing, Lucy?*

"I guess I'll never live that one down, huh?" He laughed.

"Nope," I teased. "But sure, ask me whatever you want."

"Why are you here?"

I narrowed my eyes. "What do you mean?"

"You don't need to be set up with any of these goons. Men must flock to you without Maggie's help."

My cheeks warmed. "You'd be surprised. Sometimes I feel like I have the opposite effect on men. At least the right ones."

"Well, then they're intimidated."

"Why do you say that?"

"Have you looked in the mirror lately, Snow?"

Tucker thinks I'm attractive. That doesn't mean he doesn't think of me like a sister, though.

He cleared his throat. "Anyway, I thought you were with some guy for ages."

"I was. But then he ghosted our relationship, deciding to take a job overseas."

"Damn. I'm sorry. Better to know now that he wasn't the one rather than later, though, right?"

"I guess, yeah." I shrugged. "But I'll be thirty next month, and still can't help feeling like I wasted a lot of good years on him."

He leaned his gorgeous tattooed arms against the counter. "Thirty is super young. You have your whole life ahead of you."

"Says the true youngun in this equation."

"Not that young anymore, Snow," he said with a glimmer in his eyes.

I can see that. Way too clearly right now.

"Hey!" Maggie called from behind me.

I turned. "Hey there."

"Where's your date?"

"Probably off fucking an Excel spreadsheet," Tucker cracked.

I chuckled. "It didn't work out."

Maggie frowned. "He left?"

"Well, only after I excused myself to take care of a family emergency that never actually happened."

Her eyes widened. "You lied and blew him off?"

"He was boring as hell, Maggie. I'm sorry."

She crossed her arms and huffed. "Aw, man. I thought he'd be great for you."

I rattled the ice in my drink. "I'm thinking the matchmaking thing is not for me."

"Nonsense." She smacked the counter. "I've already got someone in mind for you tomorrow night. And I promise to get it right this time."

After she left, Tucker leaned in and whispered, "You know where to find me if you need to send an SOS."

The feel of his breath on my skin gave me goosebumps. And he smelled so freaking good. The way my body reacted? It seemed to want a lot more from him than *just* an SOS. *Damn it.* Was I really lusting after Tucker? *He's Maggie's brother!* I could never.

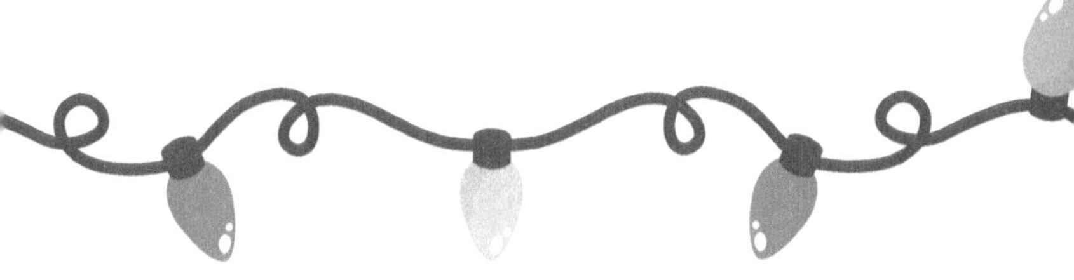

CHAPTER 3

Tucker

"What's pissing you off today?" Caleb, one of my regulars, turned around and looked straight at the booth Lucy was sitting in before turning back to me.

My eyes narrowed. "What are you talking about?"

He shrugged. "You've been shooting daggers at those two for the last hour."

"I have not." *It's been more like an hour and a half.*

"Uh-huh."

I guess I needed to cool it. But the last four nights of having to watch Lucy on dates with a bunch of douches hadn't been fun, and tonight's was especially difficult to watch. Every other evening, Lucy had looked bored as shit. The only time she'd perked up was when I raised the signs I'd made for her. But tonight she hadn't looked my way all evening. She was too busy laughing and doing the things she did when I flirted with her—blushing, running her finger along the base of her wine glass to avoid eye contact, and playing with her hair.

Caleb lifted his beer to his mouth and smirked. "You're doing it again."

Fuck. I was. "I'm just keeping an eye on my sister's friend. The guy she's hanging out with seems like a real douche."

"Oh yeah? What makes him a douche?"

I shrugged. "Side-parted hair, that stupid I-work-on-Wall-Street zip-up vest, teeth that are too white and too perfect."

Caleb's smirk widened. "Hot for your sister's friend, huh?"

"Just watching out."

"There's watching out and then there's watching. You're doing the latter, my friend."

I waved him off and went to turn down the annoying music my sister had put on. If I had to hear Mariah Carey sing "All I Want for Christmas is You" one more time, I might break a speaker. Between the decorations, my hands being sticky from tonight's *crushed candy cane brim martini*, and the same holiday tunes on repeat, I felt like I was going out of my mind.

On that note, I looked over at Lucy again, just as she threw her head back in laughter. *Yeah, it's the Christmas crap that's making me pissed off, not watching this shit.*

A little while later, I refilled Caleb's beer.

"You know," he said. "I used to have a pretty big crush on my best friend's girl."

I shrugged. "Oh yeah? Did you make a move?"

He shook his head. "Nope. Bro code. I spent five long years watching him not appreciate the good thing he had. Eventually they got engaged, and then I watched him break her heart when she caught him cheating a month before the wedding."

"Damn. That's tough. Do you still keep in touch with her?"

Caleb smiled and lifted his left hand, displaying a shiny, gold wedding band. "Every night when I get home. After they split, I woke up and took my shot. I finally realized I didn't want to live with regret and grew some balls."

His story hit home, though when I looked over and considered whether it was finally my time to take a shot with Lucy, her date was holding her damn hand across the table.

It was another half hour before he left, and I was put out of my misery. At least she hadn't gone with him. Lucy came over and sat at the bar, like she had each night this week, but I kept my distance until she finally waved me over.

"What's up?" I asked.

"Nothing. I just wanted to say hi. You've been busy."

"Hi." I pointed to the nearly empty wine glass she must've brought with her from the table. "You want another?"

She shrugged. "Sure, why not."

I poured her usual and set it on a coaster, then proceeded to wipe down the bar around her without saying anything.

"Is everything okay?" she asked.

"Why wouldn't it be?"

"I don't know. You seem...off."

"Everything's just peachy."

Lucy's brows pulled together.

I didn't have an excuse for being a jerk, so I thought I should at least make an attempt at conversation. "I guess you liked this one, huh?"

She shrugged. "He was a nice guy, but..."

"But what?"

"I don't know. Something was missing."

"Like...?"

"I'm not really sure. On paper, he checks all the boxes—good job, funny, handsome, doesn't live with his mother at thirty years old."

"Feelings don't come from checked boxes."

"I guess." She shrugged again. "Maybe it was just my mood. I think I'll go out with him again to see."

I clenched my teeth so hard, it gave me an instant headache. "You can't force chemistry to exist where it doesn't any more than you can force it to not exist where it shouldn't." I met her eyes. "Trust me, I've tried."

And then there were three.

Caleb, Lucy, and I were the only ones left in the bar at closing time. Lucy usually took off before now, though her sticking around tonight had cooled the anger I'd felt earlier.

I headed to the front window and clicked off the OPEN sign. When I turned back, Caleb was getting up from his stool. "You have a good night, Tuck." He patted me on the shoulder as he passed and lowered his voice. "Remember, don't live with regrets, man."

I walked around the bar and locked the register. "You want another glass of wine?"

"I should probably get going," Lucy said. "I can't believe I stayed out this late on a weeknight."

I nodded toward the door. "Come on, I'll walk you home."

Flurries started almost as soon as we walked out. Lucy smiled. "This is the first snowfall of the season."

"I guess it is."

"Quick, close your eyes. If you make a wish as the first snow starts falling, it's supposed to come true."

I watched as Lucy closed her eyes. A devious smile crept over her face before she opened them again. "Did you just wish for something dirty, Miss Snow?"

"No!" she said waaay too quickly.

"Uh-huh."

"How about you? Did you make your wish?"

I shook my head. "I wasn't sure if it was only the first person's wish that would come true. I didn't want to beat you to it."

She smiled. "Aww...you're even a gentleman with snowflakes. That's sweet. But I don't think it's limited to one person. So go ahead, make a wish."

I closed my eyes and asked the gods of snow for something I'd wanted for a very long time. After, I pulled up Lucy's hood, and we started on our way.

Lucy's house was about a quarter mile from the bar, in the opposite direction of mine. But the houses we'd grown up in were right next to each other. In fact, we had to pass the street we used to live on during our walk.

When we arrived at the corner of Cherry Lane, I pointed. "Want to take a detour? Pass our parents' places?"

She smiled. "Sure. I haven't gone by my mom's house since she moved to Florida three years ago."

"Same. I haven't been down this street since I loaded the U-Haul to move my parents to the condo they live in on the other side of town."

We slowed as we came to houses 404 and 406. "Want to know a secret?" I asked.

"Who would ever say no to that question?"

I chuckled. "I guess not too many people."

"What's your secret?"

"Yours was the first boob I ever saw."

"What? How?"

I pointed up to what used to be my bedroom on the second floor of my parents' house. "My room had a direct view of your yard, of your *pool*. One day, I was looking out the window, and you were getting out of the water. Your bikini top shifted as you climbed out. I saw your boob. The left one, to be exact."

Lucy laughed. "How old were you?"

"Eleven."

"Did you like what you saw?"

"I still remember it, don't I?"

She chuckled. "That means you owe me a peek at one of your body parts."

"Happy to oblige, Snow. Happy to oblige."

A few minutes later, we arrived at Lucy's place. It was decorated with strings of very uniform white lights and a simple wreath on the door. "Your house looks nice. You should've decorated the bar instead of my sister."

"It sort of looks like someone vomited Christmas in there, doesn't it?"

Lucy unlocked the door, and then there was an awkward moment. It felt like the end of a date, and I should kiss her goodnight.

"Well..." She looked down and ran her foot along the doormat. "Thanks for walking me home."

"Anytime." I leaned down and kissed her cheek, then moved my mouth to her ear. "And let me know what body part you decide you want to see. Ball's in your court. I'll be waiting."

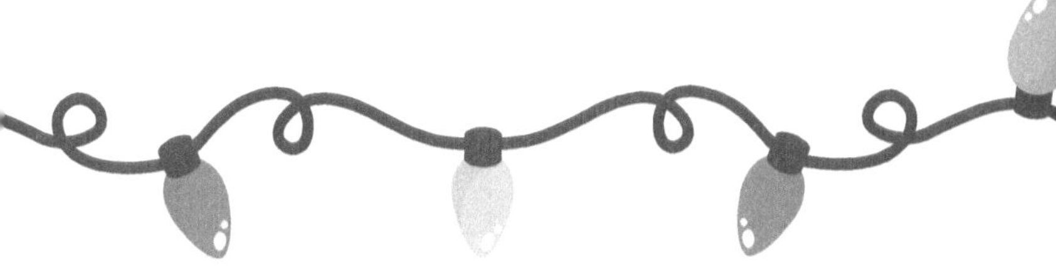

CHAPTER 4

Lucy

Ihadn't been able to concentrate at all during this dinner. It was my second date with Lorne Mitchell, a Manhattan psychiatrist. Everything had been going great, except that my mind kept wandering to whether I should stop by The Rusty Nail after.

That was certainly not a good sign for Lorne.

My date put his fork down. "Is everything okay? You look like you're not enjoying the food."

"Oh no. Everything is perfect. Sorry. My mind is on… one of my clients," I lied. "I have a hard time not taking work home with me."

"I get it. We have that in common, I think. My patients get in my head a lot, too."

This was the first time I'd been out with someone who was also in the mental-health field. I'd hoped that commonality would make things more interesting, but any small bit of chemistry between Lorne and me had fizzled since our first date.

All I could think about was what Tucker had said to me the last time we were together. *"Let me know what body part you decide you want to see. Ball's in your court. I'll be waiting."*

The pathetic thing was, I still couldn't be sure whether Tucker was serious or not. And even if he was, it still didn't imply that he wanted a serious *relationship*. I couldn't risk my friendship with Maggie for a quick tryst with her brother. *Her brother!* Oh my God. How would she even react to that? I really needed to forget what Tucker said.

But that was easier said than done.

After I parted ways with my date, I decided to stop by the bar. Tonight's dating event was likely wrapping up, and I told myself I was going to check in with Maggie. But deep down, I knew what had really brought me here was the possibility of seeing Tucker. Maybe seeing him tonight would give me some clarity.

Unfortunately, when I entered, an attractive girl had leaned in to flirt with him over the bar. *Of course.* This was Tucker's life—a hot bartender who probably took women home left and right. Women closer to his age and not four years older. Women who *weren't* his sister's best friend.

After using the bathroom, I decided to sneak out without saying anything to him.

On the drive home, I felt dumb for having stopped at the bar. It felt desperate.

Back at my place, I washed off all my makeup and changed into some comfortable clothes. Just as I was about to turn on the TV and escape into a show, there was a knock at the door.

I opened it and was surprised to find Tucker standing there. It was only ten, and the bar shouldn't have closed yet.

My breath hitched. "What are you doing here?"

His eyes traveled down to my breasts. I'd taken my bra off.

"Why did you leave the bar?" he asked, walking past me and into my house.

"You saw me?"

"Yeah. I saw you leave the bathroom and walk right out the door."

"I came to say hello to you, but you seemed...busy."

"Busy because I was working and talking to a patron, like I do every night? You made the wrong assumption."

"How are you even here, and not there? You're not closed yet."

"I had someone cover for me, Lucy. I'm the boss. I can leave whenever I want."

"You left early to come talk to me?"

"Didn't you leave the bar early, too, when you came to talk to *me*?" His eyes veered downward again, and I covered myself with my arms.

"You just ended my peepshow," he said, his voice a growl.

I cleared my throat. "Yeah, well, I'd be wearing a bra if I'd known you were coming by."

"If you answering the door with no bra is what I get for stopping by unannounced, I might plan more impromptu visits." He winked. "I'm kidding." He muttered, "Sort of."

I lowered my arms and walked over to grab my hoodie draped over the back of a chair. "I did want to see you," I admitted as I zipped it up.

"Did it have something to do with a certain decision I asked you to make the last time we were together?"

My body tingled at the mere thought of his naked body. "I'm confused about what to do with you."

"I have an idea of what you can do with me."

I rolled my eyes. "I can't tell if you're serious. But even if you are, I need more than just, you know..." As much as it seemed I *did* want that with him.

He cocked his head. "You think I'm only after one thing?"

"That's *one* of my fears when it comes to you."

"I'm sorry if I spooked you by being forward. That's just my personality."

I raised a brow. "So you do this with everyone?"

"No. Not at all. But if I want something, I try to make that clear. Not sure how I can be any clearer."

"Okay then. I'm not looking for a relationship that's purely physical."

"You're not looking for fucking amazing sex with someone who has the utmost respect for you?" He inched closer.

My body was on fire as I looked down at his strong, tattooed arms. Despite the arousal burning through me, I managed to say, "I'm not *just* looking for sex."

"And what makes you think that's all I want?"

"I don't know. I just assumed—"

The doorbell rang.

"Shit," I muttered.

Tucker's eyes narrowed. "Who's that?"

I peeked out the window to see Maggie's car outside. "It's your sister," I said, heading toward the door.

"Fuck."

I opened. "Hey." I let out a shaky breath as I ran a hand through my hair. "What are you doing here?"

"I came to see how your date went, since I was on my way home." She noticed Tucker. "What are *you* doing here?"

Tucker looked over at me and proceeded to lie. "I followed Lucy home from the bar to make sure she was okay because I noticed this weird dude leave right after her. I got paranoid that maybe he was following her."

"Oh shit. That's scary." She turned to me. "Are you okay?"

"Yeah." I exhaled. "False alarm."

"Unfortunately, it's another weird dude she has to be more concerned about..." He winked at me.

"Huh?" Maggie looked confused.

I shot daggers at Tucker.

"Wait. Why were you at the bar tonight, Lucy? I thought you were on a date with Mr. Side-Part. Lorne?"

"I was. I stopped by after."

Maggie frowned. "The date was a dud?"

"Yeah, kind of. Lorne is a great guy. But I wasn't into him. We used all our spark on the first date."

"Darn it. I was sure he was the one." She sighed. "Well, once again I'm gonna have to work even harder to find you a match."

I looked over at Tucker and noticed his sullen expression. "I'll have my marker ready," he said with a sigh.

CHAPTER 5

Lucy

Tucker hasn't looked my way once.

The following week, Maggie's Twelve Dates of Christmas fiasco was almost at an end. I hadn't heard from her since the night she'd stopped by my house and found Tucker, so I thought—no, I *hoped*—that meant she was done trying to fix me up. But no such luck. This afternoon she'd texted me to be at the bar at six o'clock. She said she'd found the *perfect* guy for me. *Again.*

I tried to say I had to work late and couldn't make it, but she just made the time later. Two other excuses hadn't worked either, so here I was, on a date with Patrick Hastings—a dentist from the Upper East Side. He was nice enough, but I found it difficult to concentrate on the man in front of me when a certain other man was behind the bar twenty feet away.

Tucker had been ignoring me all night, yet I glanced over at the bar again, only to find him talking to three attractive women. I forced my attention back to my date and managed a smile. "So, Patrick, tell me something about you that you usually wouldn't tell a woman on a first date because it's embarrassing."

Patrick sipped his beer. "I'll tell you, but you can't look at me differently after I do. Normally, I wouldn't leak this type of sensitive information until at least the fourth date—when I've had a chance to lift something heavy, maybe grill something for you, and grow some facial hair."

I smiled. "Noted that you're macho with oodles of testosterone. But go on. You have me curious now."

My date hung his head. "I cry at weddings. I can't freaking help it."

I chuckled. "Did you cry watching *The Notebook* too?"

He shook his head. "I'm not answering that. You owe me. What's something you wouldn't normally tell a guy on your first date?"

I tapped my lip. "Oh, I know. I'm obsessed with magazine quizzes."

"That's not too embarrassing."

"It is if you *really* believe in them. I used to quiz every guy I went out with during our second date."

"Used to? You don't do it anymore?"

I shook my head. "I stopped because if the guy's total points didn't land him in the category I wanted, I mentally ruled him out and started finding things wrong with him. It made it impossible to go on a third date. But I do still carry the quiz folded up in my wallet, for some ridiculous reason."

Patrick spread his arms along the top of the booth. "Pull it out. I'm up for the challenge."

"That's probably not a good idea."

"Not to be too cocky, but I'm confident I'll land right where you want me. I've felt chemistry since the moment we sat down. I'm not usually wrong about these things."

"I don't know…"

"Come on. I told you I cry at weddings, and you're still sitting here. I think we can weather a magazine quiz."

"All right…" I dug into my purse and pulled out a folded-up copy of my favorite *Cosmo* quiz. It was short and simple. "Question number one. Which answer most closely matches your ideal date?

A. Netflix and chill.
B. Going to a movie with a gallon of buttery popcorn.
C. A hike that ends at a pretty stream.
D. Clubbing."

Patrick rubbed his chin. "I spend too much time indoors working, so I'd have to say C."

I typed his answer into my notes app and read question number two. "Your date cooks you dinner, and it tastes disgusting. You…

A. Eat every bite.
B. Be honest and take her out to an amazing restaurant.
C. Eat a little bit and apologize that you had a big lunch and aren't hungry.
D. Dump her. You need a woman who can cook."

Patrick laughed. "Has anyone ever picked D?"

"You'd be surprised…"

He smiled. "I'd probably do C."

I noted his response again and continued. "Question number three. If you could have one superpower, what would it be?

A. Flying.
B. Teleporting.
C. Reading people's minds.
D. Talking to animals."

"This is a hard one," Patrick said. "I think it could be A, B, or D. Not sure I'd want to read people's minds. That sounds like a recipe for disaster."

"You can only pick one."

"I guess I'd go with B. I really like to travel."

I could tell from his first three answers that he was not going to score well. Yet I soldiered on. "Number four. What is your love language?

    A. Physical touch.

    B. Words of affirmation.

    C. Acts of service.

    D. Gifts."

"Probably acts of service."

"All right. Last question. Which kiss is your favorite?

    A. In the middle of an argument.

    B. Outside in the rain.

    C. During sex.

    D. After saying I love you."

Patrick chose C, and then I tallied up his results. "You scored an eleven."

"Does that put me in the winner's circle?"

I offered a conciliatory smile. "No. You'd have to be seven points or under."

"Oh man..."

I laughed. "It's okay. You actually got one of the lowest totals out of everyone I've ever quizzed. I'm not sure there is such a thing as a man who can score a seven or under."

An hour later, I yawned and said it was time for me to call it a night. Patrick offered to walk me home.

"Umm..." I glanced over at the bar. "Would you excuse me for a minute, please? I just need to check on something."

"Of course."

Patrick stood when I got up from the table. What a shame I didn't feel a spark. He had such nice manners.

"Hey, Tuck." I leaned my elbows on the bar and tried to sound casual. "Do you know if Maggie left?"

"Yep. About a half hour ago."

Of course I already knew that, since she'd stopped by my table to say goodnight. But I'd been invisible to Tucker all evening, so he wouldn't have noticed. Plus, I didn't care if he did at this point. Him ignoring me had gotten under my skin, and I felt the urge to make him bristle.

"Oh, okay. I was just going to say goodbye before I *left with my date.*"

Tucker's jaw flexed. I saw it! Yet he turned his back and started unloading glasses from a crate. Heaviness settled in my chest. Though...maybe he was trying to be respectful because I was, after all, on a date. Perhaps I needed to open the door for him a little.

"What about you?" I asked. "Are you leaving soon? If you are, maybe I can wait and we could walk together. Save my date the trip."

Tucker's eyes lifted to meet mine. He held my stare for a few long seconds, but then looked away, shaking his head. "I have to work late. You have a good night, Lucy."

I felt deflated the entire walk home. If Patrick noticed, he didn't say anything. When we arrived at my house, he took both my hands and asked if we could see each other again. I agreed, though I knew I'd probably blow him off when he called. There just wasn't chemistry, and of course, he'd scored an *eleven* on the stupid test.

Which reminded me...had I taken the quiz page with me? Once I was inside the house, I rummaged through my purse looking for it. I remembered folding it when we were done, but that was the last thing I could recall before talking to Tucker. I must've left it on the table at the bar.

Maybe I should go back and get it? I'd had that test in my purse for years.

No. You don't need it. The only reason I wanted to go back is to see you know who.

I forced myself to take off my coat and shoes and sat down on the couch to relax. But my neck was full of tension, and my skin felt too tight. I kept replaying how Tucker had barely looked at me all evening. Instead of winding down, I felt all revved up. After thirty minutes of telling myself I wasn't going back to The Rusty Nail, I stood abruptly, heart thudding, and grabbed my coat.

Tucker wasn't behind the bar when I walked in. So I went back to the table I'd been sitting at to see if I could find my stupid magazine quiz. It was still there, though it was no longer folded up like I could've sworn I'd left it. I grabbed the paper and started to bend it at the crease in the middle, but I stopped when I noticed that someone had circled answers on it. I always wrote my date's answers in my notes app, not on the page. A quick tally made my heart race. *Six points!* Someone had scored a six! Could it have been Tucker? I desperately wanted it to be him.

Joe, one of the guys who worked a couple of nights a week, was refilling a peanut bowl when I walked over to the bar.

"Hey, Joe. Is Tucker in the back?"

He shook his head. "He left. Went home."

"How long ago?"

"Maybe forty-five minutes."

My heart sank. Tucker had told me he had to work late. He'd lied, just so he didn't have to walk me home.

I felt my eyes filling, and suddenly, more than anything, I wanted to be back home. I swallowed and held out the paper in my hand.

"Thanks. Can you throw this out for me, please?"

He looked down as he took it. "What is it?"

"Just something stupid."

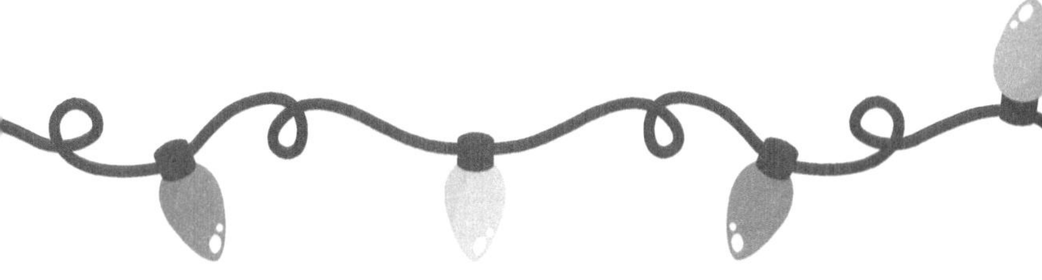

CHAPTER 6

Tucker

When I entered, the café was all done up in holiday lights. Things had been so busy lately, I hardly remembered that Christmas was only a few days away.

I'd told Maggie to meet me here for coffee. Even though what I needed to talk to her about was pretty straightforward, I found myself a bit anxious.

"What's up?" she asked as she sat down at the table after ordering herself a latte. "You never ask me to meet you for coffee."

"Why do I need an ulterior motive to want to hang with my sister?"

She narrowed her eyes. "Tucker..."

"All right..." I conceded.

"What is it?" she asked, taking a sip.

"Feel like setting me up with someone?"

"Really? You've never had trouble getting dates. Don't get me wrong, I love a challenge. But why do you need my help all of a sudden when you've done nothing but make fun of matchmaking?"

"It's not exactly about needing a date…"

Maggie crossed her arms. "Okay, then. What's going on?"

I swallowed. "I want you to make me *Lucy's* date at the next event."

She leaned back in her chair. "Lucy…?"

"Yes."

"As in my *friend* Lucy, who's four years older than you?"

"Correct, but why should the age difference matter?"

"It doesn't, except that I know Lucy is ready for a serious relationship, and I don't think that's something *you've* ever been after."

I ran my thumb along the side of my cup. "Maybe not with other people. But I'm interested in that with Lucy."

"Wow." She laughed. "I'm sorry. I wasn't prepared for this. I've already selected someone for her tonight I think she might like."

"No offense, sis, but how many times have you said that? You've had no luck finding someone for Lucy. Maybe you don't know what she needs."

"Oh really?" Maggie cocked her head. "And what exactly do *you* think she needs? And don't tell me you're packing it in your pants."

I shook my head. "It's not about that. You've been trying to find guys who look good on paper. Lucy doesn't want that. She wants someone who excites her, who makes her feel something. And that doesn't always come in a predictable package."

"Well, it doesn't get any more *unpredictable* than you, little brother. I will tell you right now, I didn't see this coming, even after I got a weird feeling the night I found you at her house."

"Nothing was going on that night. But I did lie about my reason for being there—no one was following her. Not sure why I felt the need to do that."

She arched a brow. "So, you went over there to what... seduce her?"

"I've been trying to get her to like me as more than a friend recently. But she's been reluctant to entertain my advances. I think partly because she thinks you'll be weirded out. But also, she has the same doubts about me that you do."

"There's only one way to prove us wrong, but that's going to take time, if you're serious."

I nodded, and the more I thought about the dating event tonight, the more I got a different idea. "Look, how about this. You don't need to *set her up* with me. You don't even have to approve of this. All I'm asking is for you to *not* fix her up with any other dudes until I can properly shoot my shot."

"I thought you said you already made a move?"

I rolled my eyes. "I should probably come up with something a bit more eloquent than asking her to choose which body part of mine she wants to see first."

My sister's mouth dropped open. "You didn't..."

"Have you met me?" I chuckled. "It was all in good fun, though."

She sighed. "You expect her to take you seriously when you're pulling stuff like that?"

"I'm gonna take a different approach this time."

"I'd say *anything* other than your previous approach is a step up."

I scratched my chin. "Okay, so one more favor besides not setting her up."

"What?"

"I need you to postpone the event that was supposed to be at the bar tonight. But don't tell Lucy. Let her show up at the bar."

That evening, my heart pounded as I waited. For all I knew, Lucy wouldn't show. But if she did, tonight was going to go one of two ways: really great or really bad. I couldn't imagine there being any in-between.

The door to the bar finally opened.

When Lucy walked in, she looked hotter than ever in a tight, snakeskin-patterned dress that hugged her in all the right places. Either she was trying to impress her date tonight or trying to *kill* me.

She looked around, bewilderment on her face. "Where is everyone?"

"Why, what were you expecting?" I tried my hardest to maintain my poker face.

"I'm here for my last date. The final Twelve Dates of Christmas event was supposed to be tonight, which I'm sure you already know. So why is no one here?"

"What are you talking about?" I drew my brows in, trying to hold back laughter. "People are here."

Her gaze moved around the empty bar again. "What?"

I tilted my head. "Are you losing your mind, Luce?"

You could hear a pin drop as she tried to make sense of the situation.

Lucy put her hands on her hips. "It's just you and me here. I think *you're* the one losing your mind."

"Look..." I pointed to the empty tables. "There's Maggie over there, schmoozing one of her clients." I moved my pointer finger to the other side of the bar. "And there's your boring-as-fuck date waiting for you to arrive." I turned to her. "You're late, by the way."

She blinked. The look on her face was freaking adorable. I wondered if for even a moment she considered whether I was for real.

Lucy blew a breath up into her hair. "Seriously, Tucker, what the hell is going on?"

"Nothing…"

"Tucker!"

"Are you getting pissed at me?" I grinned.

"Yes!" Her face reddened.

"Good." Wrapping my hands around her cheeks, I went in for the kill, pressing my lips against hers and taking her beautiful mouth in mine.

When Lucy moaned, I felt the vibration down my throat. Her muscles loosened with each second, tension replaced by surrender. Our tongues collided as our bodies pressed together. When I felt her starting to pull away, I brought her in closer. Her moan was even more pronounced as she once again relaxed into me, wrapping her leg around my thigh, practically trying to climb me.

When I let go, Lucy looked up at me in a haze. "What was that?"

"Everyone knows the best kind of kiss is one in the middle of an argument, Luce." I winked.

Her mouth fell open. "The quiz…"

"I had to find a way to get you mad, so I could kiss you. Making you wonder whether you were going insane was the best I could come up with."

Her expression softened. "You were the one who filled out the quiz?"

I nodded. "How did I do?"

"Better than anyone ever has." Her mouth curved into a smile.

"Let that be a lesson."

"In what?" She brushed her fingers over her swollen lips.

"I'll be the best *you* ever had, Lucy."

"You closed down the bar to kiss me?"

I inched closer. "I closed down the bar and canceled the event so we could be alone and talk. The kiss was part of the plan, yes. But the fact is, I don't want anyone else to date you. I want to officially throw my hat in the ring. Because I think you're amazing."

"Is it just physical?"

"No, it's not *just* physical. How can you think that?"

"Well, the whole...body-part-choice thing, maybe?"

"Forget about that for a second." I sighed. "Sure, I've had a crush on you from the moment I can remember being attracted to girls, but it's so much more than that." I paused as I thought back to a core memory. "When we were younger, you cried when my cat died, despite the fact that not a single person in my family shed a tear. I knew then that you were special. I could go on and on about why I like you because I've had a front-row seat to your life."

"Feel free to elaborate, then." Her eyes twinkled.

"You're kind, warm, and funny as all hell even when you don't mean to be." I shook my head. "I never thought that ex of yours was good enough for you. You're the whole package, Lucy. And I want my chance. This feels like the right time to finally shoot my shot. Will you be my date tonight?"

Her chest heaved, and she smiled. "The way I feel when I'm with you lately is different from anything else. It doesn't surprise me that you scored so well on that test, but even if you hadn't... I'm not sure it would matter at this point."

Yes. "Come sit," I said, walking her over to a table in the corner where I had some specially curated items laid out.

She sat, a look of complete and utter shock on her face. "What's all this?"

"Well, I thought I'd surprise you with some of your favorite things."

"How did you even know I liked this stuff?"

"Because all those years when you were writing me off as someone too young for you, I was paying attention."

Arranged on the table were items I knew she loved: old Nancy Drew mystery books, her favorite Gobstoppers candy, and pink peonies. Thrown in for good measure was a nostalgic photo of her and Maggie on Halloween, with me as the third wheel dressed as Batman off to the side. And then she noticed the coolest part.

"Holy crap. That's the bright pink Stanley I waited in line two hours to get, only to find they were sold out." She lifted it. "I hate to interrupt this romantic moment, but how the *hell* did you score this?"

I grinned. "Heard you talking to Maggie about missing out on it. I know a person at the store. They'd kept some in the back, so I had him snag one. I was gonna give it to you for Christmas no matter how things played out between us."

Her mouth dropped open. "I can't believe you did all this." She looked up at me. "But it's not about the stuff. It's about the fact that you remembered the details."

"I didn't want you to think my attraction to you was only about sex."

"Just to clarify, I'm not opposed to sex." She winked. "In fact, I wouldn't even be opposed to sex *tonight*."

Fuck yes. My dick twitched. "Well, okay, then. You know, I'm starting to think it's time to lock up the bar." Lucy stood from the table, and I wrapped my arm around her and kissed her forehead.

"What do you think Maggie will say about all this?" she asked.

"She knows."

Lucy's eyes went wide. "She knows?"

"Of course. How do you think I managed to postpone the event? I had to tell her the truth."

"How did she react?"

"She gave her blessing, as long as I was serious. She said to tell you she doesn't understand how her snotty-nosed brother could possibly make you happy, but if it works out, she's still giving herself indirect credit for matchmaking."

"That sounds like Maggie." Lucy reached up on her tippy toes to kiss me before I lifted her up. She wrapped her legs around me again as we fell into a kiss. "Let's get outta here," she muttered over my lips.

I didn't put her down, just stopped to grab our coats. As I carried her out of the bar, I said, "Remember that wish I made when it started to snow on the walk we took together?"

"Yeah?"

I smiled. "It came true tonight."

THE END

OTHER BOOKS BY VI KEELAND & PENELOPE WARD

Denim & Diamonds
The Rules of Dating
The Rules of Dating My Best Friend's Sister
The Rules of Dating My One-Night Stand
The Rules of Dating a Younger Man
Well Played
Not Pretending Anymore
Happily Letter After
My Favorite Souvenir
Dirty Letters
Hate Notes
Rebel Heir
Rebel Heart
Cocky Bastard
Stuck-Up Suit
Playboy Pilot
Mister Moneybags
British Bedmate
Park Avenue Player

ABOUT VI KEELAND

VI KEELAND is a #1 New York Times, #1 Wall Street Journal, and USA Today Bestselling author. With millions of books sold, her titles are currently translated in twenty-six languages and have appeared on bestseller lists in the US, Germany, Brazil, Bulgaria, Israel and Hungary. Three of her short stories have been turned into films by Passionflix, and two of her books are currently optioned for movies. She resides in New York with her husband and their three children where she is living out her own happily ever after with the boy she met at age six.

Find out more about Vi Keeland here:

Facebook Fan Group:
https://www.facebook.com/groups/ViKeelandFanGroup/
Tiktok:
https://www.tiktok.com/@vikeeland
Instagram:
http://instagram.com/Vi_Keeland/
Facebook:
https://www.facebook.com/vi.keeland
Website:
http://www.vikeeland.com
Twitter/X:
https://twitter.com/ViKeeland

OTHER BOOKS BY VI KEELAND

Indiscretion

What Happens at the Lake

Somethimg Unexpected

The Game

Jilted

The Boss Project

The Summer Proposal

The Spark

The Invitation

The Rivals

Inappropriate

All Grown Up

We Shouldn't

The Naked Truth

Something Borrowed, Something You

Beautiful Mistake

Egomaniac

Bossman

The Baller

Left Behind

Beat

Throb

Worth the Fight

Worth the Chance

Worth Forgiving

Belong to You

Made for You

First Thing I See

Someone Knows (A Thriller)

The Unravelin (A Thriller)

ABOUT PENELOPE WARD

PENELOPE WARD is a *New York Times, USA Today* and #1 *Wall Street Journal* bestselling author of contemporary romance.

She grew up in Boston with five older brothers and spent most of her twenties as a television news anchor. Penelope resides in Rhode Island with her husband, son, and beautiful daughter with autism.

With over two million books sold, she is a 21-time New York Times bestseller and the author of over twenty novels. Her books have been translated into over a dozen languages and can be found in bookstores around the world.

Find out more about Penelope Ward here:

Facebook:
https://www.facebook.com/penelopewardauthor
Facebook Private Fan Group:
https://www.facebook.com/groups/PenelopesPeeps/
Instagram:
http://instagram.com/PenelopeWardAuthor
Twitter:
https://twitter.com/PenelopeAuthor

OTHER BOOKS BY PENELOPE WARD

The House Guest

The Rocker's Muse

The Drummer's Heart

The Surrogate

I Could Never

Toe the Line

Moody

The Assignment

The Aristocrat

The Crush

The Anti-Boyfriend

Just One Year

The Day He Came Back

When August Ends

Love Online

Gentleman Nine

Drunk Dial

Mack Daddy

Stepbrother Dearest

Neighbor Dearest

RoomHate

Sins of Sevin

Jake Undone (Jake #1)

My Skylar (Jake #2)

Jake Understood (Jake #3)

Gemini